Porty Fredrich

The Questions

Why did a faithful Yugoslavian general suddenly turn his tanks against President Tito's summer house and try to assassinate the President?

Why did a colonel from one of South Africa's oldest families plant a bomb in the offices of the General Staff?

Why did a trusted Israeli major and a respected Jordanian colonel betray their countries and lead troops into Jerusalem to establish military rule?

Why was Francis Xavier Killy, the Holy Office's most valued and trustworthy Inquisitor, planning to kill the Pope?

the Inquisitor

The Devil in Kansas

✦

Simon Quinn

A DELL BOOK

Published by
DELL PUBLISHING CO., INC.
1 Dag Hammarskjold Plaza
New York, New York 10017

The cover photograph was taken at the Monk's Court,
New York City.

The Devil in Kansas

❖

Rome

ONE

THE MAN in the cell was big. His coarse woolen robe barely met his knees, and the sleeves were inches short of his wrists. He was Black Irish, with dark hair and pale skin, and dungeon pallor looked all the more unhealthy on him. The muscles of his calves and forearms stood out like blue marble.

The grate to his door slid open.

"You are a bad penitent. After all, fifteen days for killing a man isn't so bad."

"I didn't kill him. He fell," the man in the cell answered.

"You're not supposed to talk. You have a vow of silence." The face at the grate vanished and reappeared. "Anyway, the man fell out of a plane. The food is coming. Do you want bread or water?"

Killy made a face as much at the joke as the menu.

"Ungrateful," the face at the grate sighed. "Think of the dead."

"Think of them? I'm starting to envy them."

"Shhh. Your vow. You should pass your penance in

constructive ways. Exercises, for example. Did you know that when Lenin was in jail he started every day with knee squats?"

"A fanatic."

"Shhh. You could shave, at least. You have a razor blade. I gave it to you personally, myself. Your body is a temple of God."

"Saint Francis didn't shave. Jack the Ripper shaved."

"Shhh. You have no respect for anything. The least you could do is shave for confession. You have an almost new razor, some nice cool water. A little mortification of the flesh would be good for you. Ah, you have to wait for your food. Father Romagno is here to see you, to bring some light into your dark soul."

A bolt shot open and the door creaked reluctantly on its hinges. The public and venerated areas of the grottoes were served by a dehumidifier, but not the dungeons. The jailer ushered in Killy's confessor, Father Romagno. Romagno had the Roman nose; in his cassock he always put Killy in mind of a toucan.

The door shut behind them.

Romagno thumbed his breviary. He dreaded the American's confessions. Killy's honesty was sacrilegious.

"Alberto has been treating you well?" Romagno gestured at the unseen jailer.

"Sure. Dante would have loved him."

The priest shook his head mournfully. "Such a bad attitude. And you with a murder on your soul."

"I explained in my debriefing. I threw the opium out the plane door, and the Frenchman went after it. I'm sorry he is dead and his soul cannot be saved. But if you're asking me whether I should have jumped after him to give him extreme unction, the answer is no."

Romagno rubbed his eyes, weary in the face of ob-stinacy. God worked in mysterious ways, he accepted, but Killy was more mysterious than most.

"Francis Killy."

"I'm still here."

"I know. I will take your confession now. This is the final day of your penance, your last opportunity to open your heart to the mercy of God. I pray you hold nothing back. I know we have had disagreements."

He would have liked to have said Killy refused all penance, but that wasn't the case. Sometimes, to Romagno's embarrassment, Killy insisted on more penance. But fifteen days was the proscribed penalty, and to question it was to set one's own judgement above the Church's.

Killy knelt on the stone floor. Besides the two men, the only other objects in the cell were a pallet bed, a chamberpot and a crucifix.

Saints and martyrs had hidden in the grottoes. Popes rested there after death. The faithful walked through its catacombs holding candles up to the dark. More than one Holy Father had fled through it for safety in another part of the Eternal City.

History and Romagno waited for Killy's confession.

"Forgive me, Father, for I have sinned."

"Yes?"

"I was meditating on the Frenchman when I stum-bled and, for a few fleeting seconds, dreamt about this masseuse I know."

Romagno's shoulders sank.

"She's a Swedish girl, really lovely," Killy continued. "A real blonde with a mole on her spine. She does the senator from Milano."

"Fifty rosaries. I don't want to hear any more."

"You're my confessor."

"I don't have to hear garbage. And keep your voice down. It was only a dream."

"A sin of thought."

"Don't tell me the categories of sin. Let's get to the point. Did you do the thousand Hail Marys for the Frenchman?"

"Fifteen days is a long time."

"The thousand Hail Marys—did you do them?"

"Of course."

Romagno wiped the sweat from his chin. It was a small chin, sad from having lived in the shadow of his nose.

"Do two hundred more and then you can go."

"Two hundred?" Killy's grin would have disarmed anyone but Romagno. "That's a little cheap for absolution."

"Do you even have to question your good fortune?"

"Until I know the reason."

But Romagno plunged into the benediction, only too aware that the penitent was correct and that above the grotto, in the garden of the Vatican, walked two men anxious to see the Inquisitor called Killy.

TWO

THE ROMAN SUN is a yellow diamond. After lavishing warmth on innumerable piazzas, it crosses the Tiber to the Castel Sant'Angelo on up to the city-state called the Vatican, where the sun pours out a crystalline heat over Michelangelo's basilica and the still palm trees of the Vatican garden.

Up to a century ago, all Rome was held by the Holy Father, and he lost it not voluntarily but with blood and force of arms. The Vatican City itself is a makeshift creation, a compromise between Mussolini and the Church, a retrenchment appropriately guarded by fortresslike walls. At 109 acres it is the smallest state in the world, but the Vatican remains a second government to 600 million followers.

Which was why even the United States had a personal envoy to the Pope and why the envoy was in the garden.

The envoy was Catholic, naturally, a Baltimore aristocrat and a former United States Senator. At one time the Luce publications had almost made him President, but those days were gone and his position as envoy was largely honorary, facilitating a private audience with the Pope for a party contributor or arranging a Papal decoration for a Congressman. Dimly, he perceived how much help the Vatican could be with its Communist contacts (Moscow also had its Vatican envoy), but in pinstripe lockstep with the State Department he'd never explored the possibilities. Now the situation had been thrust on him and, under the full blaze of the sun, the palm-and- oleander-lined garden felt like a griddle.

"You call your agent an Inquisitor," he said. "I thought the Inquisition was over."

"It is." Monsignor Cella smiled. He was ascetic, slim as a shadow, his white hair combed tightly back from a high forehead. "There is no more Holy Office of the Inquisition. Its new name is the Congregation of the Doctrine of the Faith. Even so, for public consumption the Congregation does not exist either. The agents are called Inquisitors for traditional reasons."

The American stopped. "That's a Jesuitical distinction."

"I am a Jesuit." Cella shrugged.

"And this Inquisitor is a priest."

"Hardly. We don't send out priests to do espionage," Cella reprimanded him. "No, he's merely a lay brother of the Militia Christi. Please, don't ask, I'll tell you. The Militia Christi is a tertiary branch of the Dominicans, who originally led the Inquisition. This tangle of orders will only confuse you. Come."

Cella took the envoy by the elbow. They left the garden and passed along the side of St. Peter's to an administration building with a rusticated wall.

"The main thing," the monsignor remarked, "is that

you need a very particular kind of agent, and we are the only ones who can supply him."

Inside, the building's small vestibule ended in a pair of double doors, the second pair soundproofed with leather padding. They crossed a spacious reception room with windows shaded by three sets of draperies, the outer curtains dark maroon and the inner ones white lace. The American envoy felt more disconnected to the outside world with each step. There had always been rumors of the Inquisition still existing. Suddenly, in the diminutive Monsignor Cella and the empty building, it was real.

After the reception room came a hall they had to walk through one behind the other. On each side were bookcases incongruously covered with chicken wire to keep the thousands of heavy, leather tomes from spilling out. Finally, they reached a small, almost bare office. Cella sat behind a plain marble-topped desk and motioned for the envoy to take the other chair. A single black crucifix adorned the walls. The envoy had been carrying an attaché case. He opened it on his lap and laid its contents—three manila folders—on his side of the desk. His hand remained on them.

"Don't you have a file for me, some information about this Inquisitor of yours?"

"No."

Bluntness was all the more powerful coming from the Jesuit.

"But I understood that we would be exchanging information. I don't think it's fair that we tell you everything we know and you tell us nothing."

"You were told wrong. We say nothing about our agents. If this seems unfair, think of it this way. You have the problem, we have the solution. Now, that is unfair. You will have to accept the Inquisitor on faith."

Cella folded his hands and waited for the American to make his decision. There was only one. The folders were pushed across the desk.

"Very good." The priest nodded. He glanced through the folders. "DeBeer is the South African. Novick is the Yugoslavian. Ah, and here is the new pair. Naherman the Israeli and Hamid the Jordanian. The biographies seem complete."

"We put them together on our own. We got no aid from Tel Aviv or Amman."

Cella nodded pleasantly at the envoy, the way a teacher would nod at a student who announced the earth was round.

"Yes, this all seems fine. And your people were quite right—all four men lead back to Kansas. Thank you, this will be adequate."

When the envoy left the papal apartments, his departure was always performed with bows from half a dozen Cardinals. With Cella, he became aware that he had already been dismissed. He found himself oddly relieved. Empty attaché case in hand, he backed out of the small, tomb-size office and walked briskly down the unlit hall.

"Kansas." He heard Cella's voice breaking into laughter behind him.

Outside, the sun was tilted over the city and the Vatican's priests were returning from their long lunch, walking or riding motor scooters across the elliptic shape of the Piazza San Pietro. Student priests—Americans in black cassocks and Germans in red—wandered to their colleges.

At the Egyptian obelisk in the center of the piazza, an inspiration struck the envoy and he turned around.

The basilica of St. Peter's rose up, filling the sky. On the right hand of the church were the papal apartments; on the left hand, the building that housed the Inquisition.

Did the right hand know what the left was doing? It was too uncomfortable a thought for the envoy to entertain for long.

THREE

DAMP FROM his shower, Frank Killy looked out his apartment window over the tenements of Trastevere, the poorest, most Roman section of Rome. Across the Tiber he could see the Palatine Hill, a tourists' maze of ruins, chalky in the sun. Each summer the foreigners came, "an occupying army," the Romans called them, and each spring the Romans prepared for them by strewing the ancient hill with broken marble so the visitors wouldn't tear down the Forum for souvenirs.

Five years an Inquisitor, Killy was still a foreigner. Worse, an American. Worse yet, what the newspapers called an espionage agent. Any number of foreign poets had been seduced by Rome, had found themselves unable to leave its sun and crumbling palaces for long. Killy would leave sunset descriptions to them. What kept him was what attracted J. P. Morgan. In New York the industrialist was hated and feared. In Rome he was an anonymous fat man with spaghetti stains on his shirt who spent his days with poor friends, arguing about fate with garlic on his breath. That's

what Rome had: the illusion that you could be anything you wanted. And if you failed, who cared?

J. P. Morgan died at the Grand Hotel in Rome. So
the only difference between Morgan and himself, Killy
figured, was that he was poor and when he died it
would be in some gutter in Berlin or Warsaw.

Well, nobody had everything.

He turned on his television. The afternoon news was
on, broadcast by a woman. She was blonde but had
dark eyes. Her nose was a bit too individual to be
classic, and her mouth was full-lipped. Her voice made
disaster into melodies, and on her lips the names of
government spokesmen sounded like lovers. While he
watched, Killy dialed his phone.

"I want to leave a message for Signorina Baiarda.
. . . Yes, I know she's on the air right now. When she
comes off, tell her Signor Killy called her and has some
information she'd be interested in. I will be at the
Piazza Navona in half an hour. She'll know where.
Grazie."

Killy felt himself coming back from the dead.

He was at the Piazza Navona first, drinking a tart
Campari when Caterina Baiarda arrived. If she'd in-
tended to be angry, she smiled instead when she saw
him. He was too big for the outside café table, like a
bluff giant set among children's furniture, aware that
he was outsized and drinking to forget the fact.

"The disappearing man," she said as she sat down
with him. Her voice was even smoother without the
translation of television tubes. "I was not going to forgive you this time. What is the information you
wanted to give me?"

"My grandmother is well."

"Your grandmother is well. This is the one you had

to rush off to see a month ago. The same one you vanish to see every other month. Tell me when she's dead, otherwise I'm not interested. What a terrible liar you are."

He filled her glass with an air of great disappointment.

"I'm glad my grandmother is not here to hear that."

"If she were, I'd pull her hair out. What is she, some nymphomaniac countess you met on the Riviera? No, you haven't got a tan. My God, you are pale. Where have you been?"

"Purgatory."

"Oh, you went home to Boston. Why didn't you just say so?"

Her laugh drew the attention of tourists wandering around the piazza. There were still some foreigners this late in September, squinting at the piazza's fountains through sunglasses. The blue Italian sky left their faces red and sore, except around their eyes, where they bore white masks when they took their sunglasses off. They all bore a national stigma: sunglass masks for Americans, sandal sores for Swedes, and raw necks from camera straps for the Japanese. And all of them reacted with shock when a living Roman statue like Caterina moved and laughed.

A breeze crossed the piazza and pressed her summer dress around her legs.

"I did miss you," he apologized.

"An Italian would have said he died each minute he was away from me. Every second was a torment. He called but my line was busy, and he wondered who I was talking to. Life was unbearable. You say you missed me. Your accent is perfect, but you'll always be an American."

Her apartment was nearby, a walk-up over the fashionable Corso Vittorio Emanuele. Killy let her go up first, waiting in the proper Roman etiquette but not waiting too long. Fifteen days was a long time.

The shades were drawn against the sun when he entered. The photograph of the senator from Milano was turned to the wall. Caterina was kneeling on the daybed, her arms back and unsnapping her bra. She dropped it on the floor. Her breasts were small, the nipples large and pink. Killy pulled his clothes off.

"And that's another difference," she commented. "Italian men fold their clothes."

As she lay back, Killy drew down her pants over her hips. He kissed the hollow next to the blonde stripe of her mound. Caterina arched her back so that he could feel the soft-hard shelf of love. And on the other side, on Caterina's spine, was a penny-sized mole.

Well, he couldn't tell Romagno everything, could he?

FOUR

CELLA REVIEWED the file before him. It was none of the ones the envoy had given him the day before. This file was in a black looseleaf book and said, in Latin:

> Francis Xavier Killy, born May 10, 1938, Boston, Massachusetts, U.S.A., last of six children of Mary Kelly Killy and Joseph Francis Killy, Sergeant, Boston Police Department. Subject baptised and confirmed: Church of Our Lady, Boston Archdiocese. Education: All Saint Parochial. Considered by fathers unruly and uncooperative, of poor academic potential.
>
> 1954, FXK attacked priest. Same year, enlisted in Army of U.S.A. with parental consent. 1956, FXK transferred to Army Intelligence, West Germany, Berlin American sector. Credited with direction of Berlin tunnel "Lebensraum." 1957, FXK demobilized as lieutenant, second grade.

The priest paused to open a drawer and bring out a

small box of papers and a soft leather pouch of tobacco. He rolled one cigarette after another while he read.

> 1957, subject matriculated Harvard University, Cambridge, Massachusetts, on U.S. Department of Defense funds. Studies: International Affairs, Languages. Graduated cum laude.
>
> 1961, employed by Central Intelligence Agency. Assigned Bonn 1963, Rome 1964, Saigon 1965. Severed agency relationship 1966. See Golden Triangle addendum."

As he read, Cella arranged the hand-rolled cigarettes in a neat log pile and added an ashtray to the desk's marble top. The Vatican souvenir stands sold illustrated snap-back boxes with wax matches, but Cella used a wooden friction match, lighting it with the nail of his thumb. An odor of sulphur tinged the air, a scent he was not unaware of. He went on to the next page.

> Psychological studies of FXK give evidence of a personality that is aggressive, inquiring, suspicious. Reacts best under stress, prefers to operate alone. Demands strong father-control figure but will challenge figure. Perfectionist with self; very high pain threshold (nine on scale of ten).
>
> Religious qualifications—few.
>
> Sexual preference—heterosexual.
>
> Special skills—interrogation, military arts, light and multi-engine aircraft.
>
> Languages—most European languages; also Mandarin Chinese, Vietnamese.
>
> Record to Date—no failures.

But there was one great failure in the FXK file and
Cella turned to it.

> Golden Triangle Addendum—the Golden Tri-
> angle of Southeast Asia (Thailand, Laos and Bur-
> ma) produces two-thirds of the world opium sup-
> ply. 1966, FXK sent from Saigon to Thailand to
> establish long-range outpost to combat Thai Meo
> guerrillas. FXK force made up of expatriate
> Kuomintang (Nationalist Chinese) troops. Out-
> post successful as threat to Meo front until
> Kuomintang forces abandoned FXK and civilians.
> FXK survived slaughter and tracked Kuomin-
> tang to Burma, where troops had gone with
> harvest. Upon threatening Kuomintang general,
> FXK ordered back to Saigon, where he broke into
> files and found agency planes (Air America) were
> helping Kuomintang fly processed opium to deal-
> ers in return for anti-Communist support. FXK
> ended agency ties following month.

There was one last page, newer than the rest of the
file.

> Note well—Subject of this file has broken into
> it and read it.

It was this as much as anything else that convinced
Cella he had the right man.

Killy arrived an hour later. The prison pallor was
gone, replaced by the usual pink that at first seemed
out of place on a big man. There was nothing babyish
about the Inquisitor's eyes. They were dark as black

marble. Cella knew about Killy's sexual activities, knew and approved. Celibacy was for priests and the FBI.

"You look fit. Penance agrees with you."

Killy sat down and glanced at the three folders delivered by the American envoy. They were spread over Cella's desk like a shell game.

"I'm ready to work, if that's what you mean. Do I have a choice of these?"

"Certainly."

Cella picked up one of his cigarettes. The hand-rolling, Killy knew, was a habit Cella had picked up as a partisan priest during the war.

"Here," Cella said as he flipped one folder open, "is the case of a Yugoslavian general, Iosef Novick. Novick was forty years old, intelligent, married, a tank commander."

"You say was."

"A month ago he led his tanks against President Tito's summer house and tried to assassinate him. It was suicidal, of course, but he almost succeeded just from surprise. Until then, Novick was a very faithful Communist."

Killy reached over the folder and took one of Cella's cigarettes. It was a habit that annoyed Cella because he knew Killy didn't smoke, the agent just liked toying with the painstakingly made creations of paper and weed.

"The Russians just gave Tito the Lenin Peace Prize. That doesn't mean they didn't put Novick up to it," Killy suggested.

"That's what the Yugoslavs think," Cella agreed, his eyes following the cigarette turning over and over in Killy's hands. "An interesting case, even if it doesn't seem to fall in our jurisdiction at first glance."

"That it doesn't," Killy remarked sadly. Belgrade was just a ferry ride across the Adriatic, and then he could be back in Rome and in Caterina's bed.

"A second case. Colonel Henrik DeBeer, age thirty-five, from one of South Africa's oldest families. Two weeks ago he planted a bomb in the offices of the general staff. He only blew up some aides, however, and because his family is well connected he was allowed to take his life."

"Even further from our jurisdiction. The Boers have their own private church."

"Very well, let's try the third." Cella was not disconcerted by his agent's lack of enthusiasm. "A Major Shmuel Naherman, Israeli, hero of the '67 war. And Colonel Mustapha Hamid, Jordanian infantry commander. Both officers in their early thirties and, like DeBeer and Novick, trusted, intelligent, well liked by their men. During your penance underground, these two enemies betrayed their countries and led troops into Jerusalem in an effort to establish military rule. Their own men ending up killing them, ending a strange tragedy, and we were able to mediate between Amman and Tel Aviv. Jerusalem does happen to be our concern."

Cella reached across the desk and took back his cigarette.

"Are military men prone to suicidal insanity, Francis?"

"Yes, and then there are martyrs."

"But martyrdom is a virtue. Suicide is heresy. The line is sometimes thin, I grant, but I don't think we're dealing with either. You see these men—" Cella pulled

the folders together,—"all these men had, besides ir-
reproachable characters, one thing in common. They
were all new graduates from the United States Army's
Command and General Staff College at Fort Leavenworth, Kansas." Cella sat back and folded his arms.
He'd always reminded Killy of a thin flame, and with
his hands hidden Cella was even more so; against the
dark wall and black cassock, a bodyless head talking.
"How do you explain that, Francis? You are American, you were in the army. What in Kansas could have
influenced four foreign student officers to commit suicide and try to take as many others with them as possible? Is it a mystery? The Americans don't know.
This strange coincidence has caught their attention
too, so they sent an investigator to Leavenworth. He
was killed yesterday and they're afraid to send another
because, you see, the war instructors can spot one of
their own kind as easily as I would see another Jesuit.
And I'll be honest with you, Francis. I don't care if the
Command and General Staff College disappears tomorrow. But I do care whether the next foreign officer
is a little luckier and does start a war and gets many
innocent people killed. Or if he is a NATO officer and
drops a NATO bomb and gets everyone killed. Some
network must send an agent to Leavenworth, and after consultation with the Americans, who are even
more nervous, it's been decided that that network
should be the Holy Office and its agent should be you."

"No."

Cella unfolded his arms. The cigarette in the ashtray
was dead, untouched except for the first puff.

"Why?"

"That's not what I was hired for. Inquisitors keep
the Pope from harm, protect priests and investigate

ecclesiastical crimes. If I wanted to play spy I could have stayed with the CIA."

"The United States cannot use the services of any ally because the English and French, to take two examples, are rotten with Russians. Besides, no ally would send another student to Leavenworth if they thought their man would come back a traitor. The Americans need the cooperation of a network that is absolutely neutral and virtually unknown, especially to their instructors. That is what the Holy Office is. We have to send a man familiar with U.S. Army procedure. That is what you are.

"I'll be more specific," Cella continued after a second. "I didn't ask you to join the Holy Office just to be a bodyguard. Any good *carabiniere* could do that. And I didn't ask you because you were an efficient agent. The West and the East produce hundreds of efficient murderers every year, agents who follow orders without sensitivity or imagination. Without a conscience."

"I don't need a conscience. That's why I have you."

"Then call it sympathy or what you will that makes you hesitate to kill another human. That's what makes the Holy Office different from other agencies. That's why you will go to Kansas, because if you don't it's very likely a great many people will suffer as a result."

"There are other Inquisitors. Arthur has been to America and Mario, too."

"You are the best." Cella said it flatly, like an accusation. He pushed the folders half off the desk toward Killy. They teetered on the edge.

"And what do you get out of it?" Killy asked.

The monsignor knew when to be honest.

"If the war college is not going to disappear, I think

it would be helpful to know exactly what the latest courses in legal slaughter are, Francis. It's always important to keep up with the competition. Napoleon once said that God was on the side with the big battalions. That's not true, but Rome likes to know who has the big battalions."

"That's better," Killy said. "You're always asking me to take you on faith, but I trust your self-interest much more."

He took the folders.

"The Swiss will help us," Cella remarked. "Our Calvinist friends would also prefer to end these disturbances. It upsets the banks. Because of their political status, you will officially be only an observer at Leavenworth, but you'll take the program like any other student."

"My contact?"

"A General Pew. He is the new Director of Allied Personnel at the school. Until you identify yourself, he won't know who you are. You have two days to study the folders and your Swiss identity. Good luck, Francis."

Killy was going out the door when Cella added in a small voice, "And if you do meet the devil in Kansas, Francis, do let me know."

The agent shut the door softly behind him and wandered down the narrow hall. The books of seven centuries of the Inquisition were on either side, all the way from the first yellowed orders of Innocent III to the records of Torquemada and confessions produced on the rack. There was more than heresy and torture; racks were filled with reports of espionage from the time when the Church was the largest secret police force in the Western World, when the Protestant

Elizabeth I's agent Christopher Marlowe was knifed in a tavern and the Militia Christi roamed Europe unanswerable to any justice but their own. The first savage bloom of the Holy Office lingered into the nineteenth century in Spain and then decayed and became a reactionary secret court for the persecution of progressive clergy. The Illich Affair was the death of the second phase of the Inquisition. Through the middle 1960s, more and more liberal priests refused to repent. Illich was the last; he laughed. Too late, the old, now-dismissed masters of the Holy Office realized they had been set up by Cella. A new kind of Inquisition was needed with a new kind of Inquisitor. The hall of books was ancient history, or so Cella said.

Killy walked through the vast, empty reception room. He asked himself often enough why he had accepted Cella's offer. At the time, Killy could have had a dozen safer ways of keeping alive—consulting for French or American arms manufacturers, running a German news service, even bartending—but the Cella offer intrigued him. Killy was an agent, that was what he did best, and he needed to know if agents could do more than supply bodies for the graves of the world. Maybe he was trying to redeem the first half of his life.

It was axiomatic in the CIA and the KGB and any other agency that an agent was a man who lived on deceit and was therefore untrustworthy; "Any agent can be a double agent" was the common phrase. An agent's bravery was masochism, a need for fear. At heart, he was a coward who would kill before thinking. Without orders, he was incapable of acting rationally and even more dangerous than useless.

That was the religion of the agencies. Cella said he wanted the exceptions, the ones who suffered from a sense of honesty, who could work without orders and dared to hesitate before killing. For an agent, Killy finally decided, it was the best of ambivalent worlds.

Besides, a dead Inquisitor got a free burial. Or so Cella said.

Kansas

FIVE

In the assembly hall were a hundred officers from fifty countries: Israelis in their open-collared uniforms, Latin Americans with dark glasses and gold braid, Asians and Africans and others from every NATO ally. On the walls were pennants of every division that had trained at Leavenworth, flags with colorful felt bolts of lightning and eagles. At the hall exit was a Remington sculpture of horse soldiers.

On the platform at the front of the hall was the man who had just introduced himself as General Pew. Crewcut, fit, capable of a tight grin, he was the picture American soldier come to life.

"It's my pleasant duty," he said, "to welcome you to the Command and General Staff College. I'll be blunt with you because that is the way we do things here. In the U.S. Army, this is known as 'the generals' college.' You can be appointed to West Point; you have to earn your way here. Only the best make it. In cooperation with friendly nations, the U.S. Army trains thousands of foreign officers and soldiers in this country. Only a handful of them come to the Command and General Staff College. You can be proud. Your countries think a lot of you or you wouldn't be here today.

"Officers who graduate from the school are called 'Leavenworths.' Exactly what does that mean? Well, Fort Leavenworth is about one hundred and fifty years old. It was first established as an outpost in hostile Indian territory. Some of that heritage is still with us today in the small statue you probably noticed as you entered. The college itself is nearly a hundred years old, starting out as the United States Infantry and Cavalry School. The first foreign officer attended it in 1894. Since then, almost thirty-five hundred foreign officers have studied here with American soldiers on their way to being generals.

"Heritage and pride. Most of our greatest soldiers have studied here. Among our foreign graduates, a dozen have gone on to become not only generals but heads of government.

"Some facts of life: A number of you will be studying with other officers that your own country may now be at war with. Don't worry. With this curriculum you won't have time to notice.

"The curriculum: Intelligence and operations. Logistics and civil affairs. Training of personnel.

"The classes are run in a candid atmosphere. You will contribute. Each of you will have a military sponsor.

"You will also have a civilian sponsor. You are in the United States, so we want you to get to know us, warts and all. That means discussions with American businessmen, visits to our campuses, to art galleries and American homes.

"Our end goal? That you can share fully in what we believe is the top military college in the world. A school that builds an officer who is alert to change, aware of his responsibilities in a dynamic world, capable of meeting problems with forward-looking solutions. And if we can create a little brotherhood between fellow officers and gentlemen, that's okay with us, too."

The orientation meeting ended in applause. A West German major in a powder-blue uniform leaned over to Killy and asked what his reaction was.

"For a while I thought he was going to ask us to vote for him."

"He's no Clausewitz," the German agreed. "When do we eat?"

The German had accepted Killy's Swiss accent. The Inquisitor settled into his role.

A gamut of American officers, the college instructors, lined the corridor outside the hall as the foreign officers passed through. The instructors were not the postcard warriors Pew was. Many were black, most had paunches. They smiled but their eyes traveled over their new students with a fierce intensity. Signs in five languages pointed the way to the mess hall. The camp photographer stood to one side, shooting pictures of international amity.

Killy put himself in the middle of the throng beside his roommate, an Indonesian colonel named Malik.

"I used to go to international Boy Scout jamborees," the Indonesian said. "Same thing."

Pew waved the hundred officers off to their meal, until the hall was empty except for himself and two of the instructors. One of the instructors was black; the other was white. The grin ebbed from Pew's mouth.

He straightened out his shoulders and gripped his hands behind his back.

The black instructor approached him. Except for the color of skin and the intelligence in the black man's eyes, the two were interchangeable.

"Well?" the general asked.

"Nothing yet, but we'll have the pictures developed immediately and check out every ID. A lot of the officers have attended lower schools here in the States, so we can discard them as possibilities right away."

"I want that ringer fingered right away." Pew chewed on his lower lip. He pushed out his chest, the khaki shirt stretching under campaign ribbons.

"Yes, sir."

"And when you know, I want that son of a bitch dead. Understood?"

The two colonels glanced at each other.

"Do you want him done in the same way our investigator was killed?" the white one asked.

"Yes," Pew answered after a moment of thought. "That way it will be a message. Very good."

He swayed on the balls of his feet; except for that, the general might have been a statue. Then he came to life with a salute of dismissal. The colonels answered it.

Pew returned to the assembly hall. He was alone amid nothing but the bright pennants, flags of courage and patriotism, thunderbolts that evoked Belleau Wood and the Ardennes, horse-head banners that had flown in Sioux Country and North Africa; he was alone but not lonely.

The two colonels strode together up the hall. Someday, they too would be generals.

SIX

PEW HAD TOLD the truth. Killy had been to war colleges in the past, but this was the best, and what he remembered from the others was already outdated. In a perverse way, he found himself enjoying his role as Colonel Jean Mainz of the Swiss National Defense Force.

So did the others. In his intelligence course there were, besides himself, Malik and Heinlein, the West German—also an Indian major and a Pakistani general, a Guatemalan and a Canadian. Not to mention an equal number of amiable American student officers.

Outside the classrooms, Leavenworth might have been like any other large American military base with its married-officers' barracks, shopping centers, putting range and, beyond its perimeters, miles of flat, empty landscape. Inside the classrooms was the paradox of lively, often brilliant education in the best methods of organizing death ever devised.

He remembered his initiation into the Army when he was sixteen, standing in a shivering line with other scared kids on the Fort Benning clay while their sergeant said, "This is a rifle. It is heavy, it is big. It is your mommy and daddy. You will oil it and keep it clean. You will sleep with it and make love to it. It's your best friend and your ticket home. Don't worry about tanks and planes and artillery. You are infantry. And when those Reds come over the hill at you, that rifle can even keep you alive. So don't worry about all the crap you're going to hear about strategy, the crap you're going to hear about C-rations, the crap you're going to hear about catching the clap at the USO. You know which end of your rifle is which and you can make it in this man's army."

That was light-years ago. Even the days in Berlin were simplistic by comparison, wondering which checkpoint the Russians would come through, tapping the East German telephone wires, sitting in the rain night after night in a Volkswagen that had a useless heater when the engine wasn't running and listening to his CIA contact grumbling that "Three days is all we get. The tank barriers will go in an hour, so we blow all the houses. An airlift? Forget it! The only thing we'll see with wings are angels."

Harvard was a summer camp. Not that the professors knew it. It was fashionable to be a hawk then. Theories about guerrilla warfare were the academic rage. A "popular" professor was willing to go "eyeball to eyeball" with the Reds and practically wore a Phys Ed whistle around his button-down collar.

And the agency. Despite all the electronic marvels everyone thought the Central Intelligence Agency could throw into the fight for freedom, when all the theories bogged down in the jungles, when the jets couldn't shoot down elephants and the technology mildewed, they sent Killy in to get one primitive Southeast Asian tribe to fight another with World War II carbines and Stone Age spears.

Leave it to Leavenworth to think ahead. He could be sarcastic about it, but Killy, alias Colonel Mainz, also had to admit he was interested and impressed.

"TRICAP is the name for what we believe is the combat division of the future," the instructor in Operations said. He was a black colonel named Jones and, from what Killy had heard, a genius and the favorite of General Pew. "TRICAP is so called because it is a division with triple capacity and the special feature of a squadron of tank-destroying killer helicopters."

"Ah, a new sort of Panzer division," the German officer spoke up.

"Precisely, and with the same revolutionary effect on warfare." As Jones talked the officers took notes. "A divisional mix of tank battalions, air-mobile infantry and armored cavalry, and killer copters. As you know, the use of attack copters evolved in Vietnam. Tests by the First Cavalry at Fort Hood in Texas have convinced us our newer attack copters will be even more useful in a 'mid-intensity environment'—that is, a war in Europe or the Middle East."

"Basically, to offset the Russian advantage in tanks?" Killy suggested.

"Yes." Jones seemed especially pleased by Killy's remark. "Their advantage in tanks and perhaps even in fighter planes. Our answer is coordination and a beast called the AH-IG Cobra. The Hood tests have shown that the Cobra is almost impossible to spot from a supersonic fighter. But each Cobra will be equipped with seventy-six air-to-ground rockets, a minigun capable of firing four thousand rounds per minute, a 40-mm grenade launcher that fires four hundred rounds per minute and TOW missiles. The TOW stands for Tube-launched Optically-guided Wire-tracked. Inexpensive and highly accurate. The Cobras will operate in platoons of three scout copters, five Cobras and one supply copter."

One of the American officers raised his hand awkwardly.

"I hate to be a wet blanket, but you were talking about coordination. Well, these copters will be going all over the place looking for tanks. They might go fifty or a hundred miles away from company command. How is the commander going to coordinate them with his ground forces?"

"A good question," Jones agreed. "Who can answer that?" He looked around.

The student officers were attentive but silent.

"Colonel Heinlein?"

The German shrugged. "You are talking about something more fluid than what a Panzer division or a blitzkrieg operation could do."

Jones went around the room until he landed on Killy.

"Colonel Mainz, somehow I think you have the answer."

Killy made a point of scratching his head before replying.

"All I can say is the only analogy I know is Swiss banks."

The tension in the class broke with jokes.

Jones hushed them. "Go on, Colonel."

"I mean, the accounts of our banks are also unusually fluid. The object is, after all, that some interested parties will not know how much money is in these accounts. So, our bankers keep track of them the only way they can—with computers."

"Bingo!" Jones exclaimed. "You know the term, Colonel? Of course not. But you're right. Part of each company command will be a battlefield computer no larger than a command radio."

The rest of the class was spent on discussion of the use of the computer in tactics. Killy was careful not to answer any more questions. All the same, Jones stopped him as the officers left at the end of the class.

"You know, Colonel Mainz, it's a shame you are Swiss. You've got all the right intuition for combat."

Killy blushed appropriately.

"You never have seen combat, have you?" Jones went on.

"I play water polo," Killy blurted out. "It's a very rough sport."

Jones pursed his lips. "Yes, I'm sure it is." But he seemed disappointed.

Killy met Jones again in the mess hall. Leavenworth's cuisine was superior. Most of the foreign officers glutted themselves on sirloins, and there were vegetarian dishes for the officers whose religion forbade meat. Killy and Malik were eating cherry pie à la mode with coffee. Jones sat down with them, smoking a pipe and exuding conviviality.

"How do you like your first day at school?" he asked as he sat at their table.

"Wonderful sales talk," the Indonesian chirped. He spoke in a soprano, Hollywood-1930s fashion. Killy was used to it by now, but Jones was surprised.

"Sales talk?"

"Sure," Malik followed up. "My brother is the biggest Honda dealer in Jakarta. It's the same sort of sales talk he gives, only better. I mean, if the TRICAP division is the army of the future, we should have it, right? The United States is the only manufacturer of Cobras and battlefield computers, right? So, the smart buyer gets a Honda and a Cobra, right?"

Unruffled, Jones puffed on his pipe.

"Right. But we give pretty good finance arrangements." He winked at Killy. "By the way, Colonel Mainz, I wanted to tell you about your military sponsor, Major Livingston. He's been called to Washington on special duty and I hoped you wouldn't mind if I took over in his place."

"Not at all."

"Fine. I'm sure we're going to get to know each other very well. See you tomorrow, gentlemen."

When Jones left, Malik let his fork drop to his plate.

"How did you manage that? Everybody wants Colonel Jones as his sponsor. He's one of the big shots here."

"Luck, I suppose."

Night ended the first full day of the war college. At a far end of the camp, American officers gathered around a floodlit swimming pool. In the office of Colonel Oliver Jones, a team of the college staff's intelligence analysts studied the records of every foreign officer.

"We can eliminate all the officers who have been in this country before," Jones mused out loud. "Then all the officers who have held NATO or SEATO or CENTO commands. Then those who are known personally by men on our staff. That cuts it down from one hundred possibilities to less than twenty."

"Well, I've been through all the pictures and the records," another colonel answered. His name was Hilliard, he was chief instructor in information gathering and was the other colonel who had received the final private orders from General Pew outside the assembly hall. "There are errors but nothing suspicious. But there are some lines of development we should consider."

Jones waited. Unlike his superior, Pew, the colonel's silence was more than statuary.

"This is Captain Rowan's area, though," Hilliard said. "He's the psychologist."

The room's attention turned to a small, chocolate-colored officer in an easy chair. Rowan was the only black officer with even the military's version of an Afro.

"There are some personality traits that we can look for. No matter how much the agent we're looking for tries to disguise himself with a new nationality or how ignorant he seems about what is taught in the classes, we will find our man is one the other officers tend to respect, even like. A natural leader, the one who would be elected class president, if you know what I mean."

"I know," Jones said. "I just became sponsor to someone like that." He felt the small tire of fat around his middle. Underneath, there was still enough muscle. Jones smiled. "Did you know that the first foreign officer ever here in Leavenworth was a Swiss?"

The colonel looked at his watch.

"Anyway, since we didn't get anything from the pictures we'll knock off for tonight. I suggest, though, that we all give short essay assignments as soon as possible and then pass some of these on to the handwriting analysts. As I remember, that's how you caught the

Russian in the typing pool at Fort Hood, wasn't it, Colonel Hilliard?"

"Yes, but that was a killer's handwriting among typists," the intelligence instructor protested. "Put one way, all the officers here are trained killers."

"No. They're bureaucrats. Organization men. Death is just the product of their organization. We're looking for the lone wolf, an agent, not an officer. There's a difference. He's on the prowl, we're following orders."

In the foreign officers' quarters, the Inquisitor was awake. Malik snored in the other bed. In the next room were Heinlein and a French officer. On the other side, two Arabs.

Killy got out of the bed and went to the window. A hundred yards away, over a dried-out lawn patroled by military police in a jeep with the headlights off, was the war college. There, among the instructors, was his target.

Killy had said he was "lucky" to get Jones as a sponsor. He wasn't kidding Malik. Jones had instructed Novick and DeBeer and Jones was sponsor to Hamid and Naherman. What better place to start?

SEVEN

NUCLEAR AND CONVENTIONAL warfare, supply logistics, civil and military administration, and intelligence gathering filled the first week of courses. Each evening Jones got together with Killy and they went over the lessons, everything the modern general should know. The rest of American life in Fort Leavenworth seemed still distant when General Pew announced that they would be having their first meeting with their civilian counterparts. On Friday night, Cadillacs and new station wagons filed in front of the foreign-officers quarters to take them into the strange world called the United States.

"First, we'll all meet at a hunting lodge and then go to the separate sponsors' houses," Jones explained as he and Killy slipped into the rear of a Fleetwood limousine.

"Who is my civilian sponsor?"

"The owner of this car, Harvey Drobski. Know the name? Well, no reason why you should, but he's about the biggest farmer in Kansas. A Russian. Farming re-

ally got started in this state when some Russian Men-
nonites came here in the 1870s and planted 'Turkey
Red.' "

"Sounds like poppies."

"Yeah, but it's winter wheat. Harvey's descended
from those first Russians, and he's about the biggest
man around now."

The limousine shot out of the fort. The flat horizon
was dimly marked by the black prairie and a dark
blue sky. The cars following one after the other might
have been a stream of shooting stars.

"This must be pretty strange to you, coming from
Switzerland." Jones lit his pipe. The fire in its bowl
gave his face a reddish hue.

"Why?"

"The Alps. You must be used to mountains."

"The center of my country is flat, though. You've
never been there?"

"No, but I'll have to try. You Swiss are pretty sur-
prising. Did you know that you're already at the top
of every class?"

It was a lie and Killy knew it; since the first day
he'd been careful to let others shine. With Jones's eyes
on him, he just looked pleased.

"Oh, it's not necessarily the answers I'm talking
about," the colonel said between puffs. "It's your
grasp of our terminology. The words and phrases you
use. They're practically ours all the time. Your grasp is
so good, you're almost American."

"That is flattering."

The two men smiled at each other. Jones looked for
one giveaway blink of hesitation. Killy had faced the
same probing smile from Russians, Chinese and Jes-
uits. He didn't falter.

"Yes, you're really pretty good," Jones said at last, letting the Inquisitor take it any way he wanted.

Fifty miles from Leavenworth, the cars took a side road from the highway. Ten minutes later, they massed in the wide, dirt driveway of a sprawling lodge. The neon sign on the roof said, "Turkey Red Inn." The sign on the door said, "Members Only."

Killy and Jones were among the last ones inside. The party had already started. A polka band was playing on a makeshift dance floor. Pakistanis, Colombians and Nigerians were being handed steins of cold beer. The Army and Drobski had done their job well. In a matter of minutes, Killy met civilian sponsors that ranged from stockyard magnates to insurance-company presidents, influential businessmen who were only too eager for the prestige of doing the Army a favor. The sponsors were also well aware that the foreign officer of today might be the President of his country tomorrow, and that sort of friendship never hurt.

Amid the laughter and backslapping, Jones pointed out other guests: the state's lieutenant-governor, an undersecretary of defense and a United States Senator or two.

"As I told you, Harvey is a pretty big man. You're lucky to have him as your sponsor."

How lucky can one man get? Killy wondered. Jones led him to the head table.

Drobski was about as Russian as cornflakes. He wore a tweed jacket and a string tie with a silver Indian slide. His pudgy hand bore a University of Kansas class ring, and Killy half expected to get the fraternity grip when they shook hands. The face on the rich man was puffed and balding. Forehead, squat nose, lips and jaw all threated to slide down into his double chins. He had great energy, however.

"Hey, this is the Colonel Mainz I've been hearing about. Meet my wife, Carla. This is my daughter, Carlotta. Come on, Jonesy, you sit down too."

Wife and daughter shook Killy's hand timidly. Mrs. Drobski had been a beauty once, perhaps Homecoming Queen at Kansas, but her looks were held together now by face lifts and elastic. The daughter, sadly, had inherited her father's porcine features.

Drobski rambled on with gusto. Flashes of insight pierced the flab. Killy recognized the type: a pig at home and a tiger in business.

"You've got to sign the inn guest register. We've got every President since Eisenhower on it and every Chief of Staff besides. Some officers who went on to big things, too. Presidents, Prime Ministers. Of course, some of them didn't work out. Like that Al-Nimiery from the Sudan. Went on to be a Red."

At a cautionary glance from Jones, Drobski changed the subject. Killy had the feeling that the colonel would have let the man ramble on the evils of Communism but that the conversation was getting too close to other officers who were more dead than Red.

"How do you like the school?" Drobski inquired. He pushed a stein to Killy.

"It's very educational."

"Well, you've got the right teacher in Jonesy. Got a little soft around the middle like me." Drobski poked Jones in the stomach. "But he was a regular killer in Vietnam. A war hero. Cheers."

Drobski gulped his beer. When he put the stein

down, a white mustache of froth circled his upper lip.

"How do you say that in Swiss?" he asked.

Damn, what do they say in Switzerland? Killy asked himself.

"To neutrality," he improvised.

Drobski, the diplomat, became serious.

"Don't take offense when I talk like a patriot. The Reds have their good points like everyone else. No one loves peace more than me."

Carla Drobski waved over a waiter and asked for a Jack Daniels. Miss Drobski requested a Whiskey Sour. The band got louder, drowning out speech. Killy escaped from the table by steering the girl around the dance floor. One drink had loosened what grip she had on herself. Her dull hair was falling out of its hairspray, her eyes became damp and her lips trembled. Killy felt he wasn't dancing so much as playing lifesaver to a sinking swimmer.

"You don't have to do this, you know," she muttered to his shoulder.

"I like to dance with you," he said and tried putting more zeal in the grip on her waist.

"You don't have to lie, either. All Daddy's officers think they have to dance with me. Ali was the only one who really did." She sighed. "Ali was wonderful."

"Who's Ali?"

"Colonel Hamid. Daddy was his sponsor. Ali was really nice. We used to dance all the time."

"Why not? You're an excellent dancer," he winced and tried to figure out how she could manage to step on his feet with her heels. 'Dancing,' he decided, was Carlotta's euphemism for something else she'd done with Colonel Hamid. No man could dance with her twice. "You must have met a lot of officers."

"Ali. There was that Israeli officer, but he was Jewish."

"Oh, I see."

"And General Novick was a nice gentleman but I couldn't understand his English at all. Colonel De-Beer was married. But the only one I really liked anyway was Ali."

They finished out the dance staggering like contestants completing the one-thousandth round in a dance marathon. On the way back to the table, Carlotta sniffed. Her emotions started at her sinuses.

"I just hope they don't get you like they did the others," she whined.

Killy grabbed her wrist.

"What do you mean by that?"

"I mean, you're nice."

He couldn't get more out of her. Drobski clapped proudly as they rejoined the table and he chucked his daughter under the chin as she slumped into her chair.

"Daddy's little girl," he said.

Daddy's little girl with the first information in a week, Killy thought with exasperation. None of the dead man's folders had mentioned their mutual civilian sponsor. Army Intelligence either didn't dare or never thought to investigate jovial Harvey Drobski.

"Need a drink?" Jones grinned.

Now what's the Swiss slang for "shove it," Killy pondered.

"That would be enjoyable," he said instead.

Killy didn't get the drink. Drobski suddenly rounded up three tables of officers and sponsors for another drive, this one of twenty miles, to his house. Cadillacs and Country Squires again unloaded a United Nations of military men as the millionaire waved his hand at what he called home.

The Drobski mansion would have been rustic if it weren't three stories tall, didn't have two wings each fifty yards long and didn't have security floodlights lighting the cozy clapboard façade with a white glare. Far away, Killy could see other floodlights trained on silos, the silos standing like missiles.

Carlotta sulkily went inside. Drobski ushered the rest behind her into a foyer a little smaller than the Astrodome. A cocktail party waited for them in the living room, a vast arena of overstuffed chairs, moose heads and an enormous oil painting of harvesters moving over a wheat field. Along with the drinks were new people to meet, more everyday American folks who happened to be mayors, corporation presidents or golf pros. The American Dream on the hoof.

Killy accepted a Scotch from the bar wagon and, while the mayor's wife conversed with his nodding head, did some calculating.

The dead men were linked to Jones and Drobski. Jones was black and Drobski was so-called Russian. So what? Jones had a very good position in the best war college and excellent chances of advancement. Drobski was a "middle American", a booster, well off and happy. What did they have to gain from conspiracies in Europe and Africa?

Jones suspected him of being an agent. Why not? The staff had already been investigated once. Jones was a trained killer. Who wasn't at Leavenworth?

All Killy had to go on was the self-pitying mutter of an unhappy girl. Even now, he saw Carlotta being taken to bed by her mother.

"Pardon?" He asked.

"I said, I always wanted to go to Switzerland since I saw *The Sound of Music*," the mayor's wife repeated.

"That was set in Austria, I believe," a goateed gentleman injected.

"There was that song about edelweiss, I remember that." She stuck to her guns.

Drobski slung his arm around the interloper's shoulders.

"This is a man I wanted you to meet, Colonel. Kelton Cero. I just about had to drag him here from the university."

Cero was a passive captive of Drobski's hospitality, a showpiece intellectual. Although his black beard came to a satanic point, Cero's shoulders were slumped and his gaze was vague. When he talked, Killy had to lean over to hear him.

"Mr. Drobski has been my benefactor," he whispered. "Perhaps you've heard of the Carla Drobski Center for Psychological Studies?"

"No, I'm afraid not. It's not my field."

"Dr. Cero is the brains behind the center. I'm just the guy who gives the money," Drobski said, unnecessarily. "Tell him about your work, Doc."

"I'm sure the colonel is not interested."

"Of course he is. Do you know—" Drobski jabbed Killy's chest— "Dr. Cero says he can cure any mental illness that exists. That's a win attitude, the kind of attitude I'll back."

"That's an amazing claim," Killy noted.

"No claim," Cero said quietly.

Killy turned away with distaste. If Drobski wanted to throw his money away on a charlatan, that was Drobski's business.

Distaste evaporated from Killy's mouth. He'd turned

to face a woman who made his whole charade worthwhile. She had the fine, oval face of a Bolshoi ballerina. Her hair was a rich black and her eyes were green and amused. In Drobski's hideous living room, she was a Siamese cat set in an alley. The smile on her lips showed that she had been listening to the conversation.

"I am Mrs. Cero," she said. Killy's hopes sank and then she added, "I could use a drink."

Killy weaved his way through the guests to the bar wagon. When he started back, he found she had followed him.

"Thank you." She looked down at the Scotch and ice and back up at Killy. Mrs. Cero was dressed no better than the rest of the women in the room. The difference was that their gowns were the total of their decoration. Hers was a blue ribbon on a work of art, a work of art that was out of reach.

"I wish Kelton wouldn't talk so much," she said.

"If he can cure anything, why not?"

"He thinks he can, you know," she answered wryly. "And if Harvey didn't give the money to Kelton it would only go to the football team. But I wish he wouldn't talk for other reasons."

"What other reasons?"

"Now he is aware that you smell a rat. He will avoid you in the future and we will not get to know each other."

A sexual invitation and a refusal all in one breath. But she was right, Killy knew. There was nothing he felt more like doing than going to bed with the charlatan's wife. It may not have fit into Cella's idea of an Inquisitor's investigation, but the Vatican was far, far away.

"What is your name?"

"Irene. Or, as Harvey puts it, Goodnight Irene."

Yes, Killy bet Harvey Drobski had let his Mennonite's eyes roam over his protégé's wife. A little bit of lust never hurt generosity, either.

"I am Jean Mainz. I'm at the war school at Leavenworth. I'm not interested in seeing your husband, but it would be a pleasure to meet you again."

She handed the drink back to him. "Colonel, thanks again. Obviously, you don't know small country communities. If I even spend another minute talking to you, the women in this room will accuse me of adultery."

"That was my intention."

"The idea has its appeal, but, again, no thank you."

She touched his hand and moved into the social mix of Drobski's guests. Her place was taken at Killy's side by Malik, who had come with his sponsor.

"That is what I came to America for," the Indonesian blurted out. "Can you introduce me?"

The little Asian's eyes danced feverishly.

"I think you're forgetting what we came here for," Killy sighed.

"What's that?"

"Make war, not love. Here, have a drink on me."

EIGHT

GENERAL PEW leaned out the open side of the helicopter and watched the entire school body of the command college spread out over the war course. Three weeks of classroom instruction had passed. It was time to put their training into practice.

Below him were companies of enlisted men and tanks. Behind them, ready to lift off, Cobra squadrons. Bulkier Huey helicopters were stuffed with airborne troops and officers. In the center was the command tent with its compact mechanical brain. Fifteen miles away was the enemy, the invading force with its larger, more orthodox blend of massed troops and shields of heavy tanks. The war game was about to start.

"Any time," the pilot shouted over the noise of the rotors as the signal came over his radio.

Pew leaned farther out, his free hand gripping a squat flare gun. He pulled the trigger and his hand recoiled back to his shoulder. A spume of red powder crossed the sky.

Killy's helicopter lifted itself backward from a whirlpool of dust. He was part of a motorcycle reconnaissance team, another feature of the TRICAP division. With him were four American officers and Colonel Jones. In a sky full of lifting choppers, he felt he might as well have been back in Vietnam.

"I hope your roommate's brother doesn't hear about these," Jones yelled.

The motorcycles weren't Hondas but Suzuki 185's, tough and nearly silent machines. According to TRICAP planners, a rider would be able to scout enemy advances, radio artillery fire in, and handle unfriendly tanks with a hand version of the TOW missile.

Killer Cobras protected the Huey as it flew far ahead of the division command. Soon, even the regular airborne troops were left out of sight. The Huey dipped down to a terrain of eroded creek beds and small hills. It stopped and hovered five feet above the ground and the first rider jumped out with his cycle.

"Remember, your main duty is recon. Don't try to be a hero just because the unfriendlies will be firing markers instead of real bullets. We want to make this simulation as real as possible," Jones instructed the remaining riders.

The Huey dipped down again and dropped its second rider. Still moving to the right flank another thousand yards, it dipped and the third rider jumped out with his machine.

"Aren't we moving out of the war course?" Killy asked. Jones ignored the question.

The Huey moved at treetop level. The Cobra cover peeled off toward the main thrust of the simulated attack. On a bluff, the fourth rider dropped to the ground and started his machine.

As the helicopter lifted up, Jones pulled his pipe from his fatigues and lit it. He threw the match out the bay. Killy watched the match spin away in the air. When he looked back, Jones was pointing a service .45 at the Inquisitor's chest.

"It's a funny thing about war games. Somebody always gets killed in them," Jones said.

"What are you doing?"

Jones moved to Killy's side, putting the agent nearer the open bay.

"You're a damn good agent, whoever you are. I had a hunch it was you, but I couldn't break your cover. None of us could. Can you guess who did it?"

The air whistled in on Killy's sweat. He clutched the side of the bay.

"I don't know what you're talking about, Colonel."

"Too bad, you guessed it once in class. The brain that's running this whole show. The computer. We tried handwriting analyses, bugged every room in the school to take apart every word of yours, went over your biography a hundred times. Got nowhere. Fed it into the computer instead and got the right answer in an hour. You see, the computer says there's no other possibility among all the other foreign officers. You're the only one who could be a free-lance operator. A simple process of elimination and all it leaves is you."

"To do what?"

"Whatever the other operators did to Naherman and Hamid and DeBeer and Novick. I don't know how you did it and I don't care. But we're going to send a message to whoever sent you not to send anymore. Not to Leavenworth."

The Huey passed over a high fence. They were definitely out of the war-games area now. Killy knew from the recon maps he'd seen earlier that they were now over the firing range.

"I could just shoot you and push you out, but we want to take care of you the same way your people murdered one of ours. General Pew likes the idea."

"He knows about this?"

"His orders." Jones paused for a puff. "His and the computer's."

The helicopter sank lower to the ground. Cella had come to the conclusion that the war-college instructors had to be responsible for the four dead officers. The instructors decided it had to be agents posing as student officers. That left Killy in the middle. And fingered by a computer.

Jones kicked the cycle and missile launcher out the bay.

"You won't need the radio. We'll put it with your body later." The ground rose up, from fifty feet to twenty-five to ten. "Any last thing you'd like to say?"

The heat of the Kansas summer made the colonel's face shine like ebony. His dull green khakis had a worn, comfortable look. The inner rib cage of the Huey was marked by stencils: PROPERTY OF US ARMY. The suction of the jet-propelled rotors took Killy's breath away. It was too much like Nam. But it was Kansas and he was being killed as the man he'd come to find.

"Nothing you'd believe," Killy said and stepped back. He dropped ten feet to the ground, rolling to soften the fall. The updraft from the helicopter blinded him and he crawled on all fours, expecting Jones to fire down. But the Huey rose and the dust settled. In moments, the helicopter was a mile away over the war-games course.

Killy stood up. The fence and the perimeter of the firing range were out of sight to the west. Nothing was in sight on the firing range except torn ground with patches of grass. He picked up the Suzuki and kicked the starter. The cycle's small engine came alive.

He got on and rode to the missile launcher. It was shorter and thicker than a bazooka. He slung the weapon over his back. Instead of a warhead, its missile carried a charge of red dye. There was no point in abandoning it; he needed everything he could get his hands on.

The ground was uneven and tortured. He bounced along it at sixty, gripping the handlebars lightly, the way he had been taught in courier training sixteen years before. The Suzuki responded, twisting around craters that gaped like the scars of a disease in the earth.

The sense of freedom was illusory. The Suzuki roared out of a depression and Killy braked desperately to a halt. The fence lay ahead, steel wire ten feet high with a **Y** of barbed wire at the top.

Between Killy and the fence, approaching him at forty miles per hour, was a tank. It was not an M60, the tank used in the war games. This one was faster and lower, a squat, black shadow swimming across the terrain like a shark through water. At two hundred yards, Killy felt the chill of identification.

The tank was the XM803, a one-of-a-kind experimental monster. Jones had described it once in class. The XM was as fast as a motorcycle, carried radar-fired Shillelagh missiles, a British 105-mm cannon, and three machine guns—two fixed and one moving. At forty tons and a cost of a million dollars, it was Tyrannosaurus Rex, legendary and uncopied because of its incredible expense.

Killy jerked the bike's front wheel to the left and took off, leaving a rooster tail of dirt. Agilely, the XM cut with him.

He felt rangefinders and radar on his neck. Killy wasn't avoiding shell craters anymore; he slewed down through every one, leaving the tank blind as much as he could. The Suzuki bucked angrily in his hands. The XM could have destroyed him already, Killy knew. The men inside it just wanted to play dinosaur and mouse.

In a long trough of dug-up earth, Killy added precious feet to his lead. As he came out, the wheels five feet off the ground, another black shark approached him head on.

There were two XMs. Killy leaned on one foot and spun away. His hand shot the bike from one gear to another. He was heading directly away from the fence now and into the heart of the firing course.

A third XM loomed up out of a crater, the barrel of its gun jutting into the sky.

"Son of a bitch," Killy heard himself saying. The Suzuki almost turned over as he planted his foot on the ground and spun the bike around again. For a monster that was supposed to be one of a kind, the supertank was multiplying too damn fast.

Killy tore up craters as he raced north, the clutch twisted as far as it would go. The XMs raced with him, raising dust clouds that towered fifty feet in the air.

"Where are you? I know you're there," Killy said through a sour grin.

On cue, the fourth XM climbed out of its crater. The trap had closed and there was no way out.

Killy clutched down, braking the bike to thirty as he veered into a circle. Dust caked on the perspiration of his face and his hands were raw. The missile launcher slammed into his back with each sudden shudder.

The four tanks moved in, diminishing the box. Killy rode in a ring, watching the flattened metal cupolas of their gun carriages. Molded into the armor were eye slits, radar and heat sensors. There would be instructors inside the tanks, men who knew what they were doing. There would be no mistakes and it was always good to keep in practice.

Killy ducked as he saw a machine-gun bubble track him. The machine-gun bubble of the next XM picked him up. The third tank's cannon swung smoothly on his path.

He jerked the front wheel back and to the side, landing on his side. Thirty feet ahead, where he would have been, the earth erupted under a 105-mm. shell. Killy heard only the first wave of the explosion; his ears went deaf after that. Among the flying rocks, he righted the bike and drove through the falling rocks. He swallowed and his hearing returned.

As Killy appeared from the dust, the tanks backed up, widening the trap but cutting off escape. Killy had to swerve from one of the moving XMs and back into the center of the ring.

There was a pause while he rode on his deadly merry-go-round. The tanks backed up farther, communicating with each other by radio. One XM rolled forward.

It would be the missile this time, Killy was sure. They had a live target and they would make the most of it. Of him. The radar pulsar of the missile's warhead couldn't miss the way the shell did; it would follow the bike as faithfully as a lover. Killy shoved the bike back up to sixty. Not that it mattered; the missile would move at ten times his speed.

The XM's carriage swiveled on its bearings. Eyes and radar noticed that Killy was slowing down. The radar was locked in and a thumb depressed a button. The missile didn't fire immediately. That was the radar's job.

From the corner of his eye, Killy saw a flash from the tank's launcher. Something new and alive was behind him filling the air with a nearly insect buzz. As he listened, time seemed to stretch, and although he knew the missile was traveling terribly fast it seemed to take forever to reach him. He dove from the Suzuki, kicking the bike in the opposite direction. The air filled with unbelievable heat.

At 600 miles per hour, the missile's radar image of Killy had suddenly split in two. Before the warhead's simple computer could choose which half to destroy, it passed between man and bike. The missile locked on a new target, an XM. The Shillelagh's course was not totally corrected, so it struck only a glancing blow at the tank, tearing out one of its treads.

Killy's legs were on fire. He beat the flames out and hobbled to the bike. The Suzuki was still running, lying on its side and wheels spinning. Killy pulled it upright and jumped on, taking off with a running start.

He headed for the crippled tank. As he passed, the men inside recovered and the gun carriage whined as it tracked him. Two heavy-caliber machine guns fired, every tenth shell a phosphorus tracer. They reached out for him, ripping open the earth. One shell hit the launcher he still carried on his back, jamming the launcher into his skull. The bike's front wheel wobbled. As he faltered, another shell hit the bike. It severed the muffler. Without it, the Suzuki screamed like a wounded animal.

Killy plunged down into a crater. The machine-gun shells passed futilely overhead. His vision cleared. The crater was one of a series, the result of an artillery pattern.

On his left, the way to the fence, new craters erupted. The XMs were firing to keep him from turning to escape. The craters came to an end, and he headed for a new series, nearer the fence. The machine guns opened up again but not in time. Killy had already vanished.

His raw legs felt the Suzuki's single piston heating to the breaking point. The second series of craters came to an end. As he roared out, he saw that there wasn't a third. The fence was half a mile away. He turned directly for it.

Two XMs were behind him. He twisted around on his seat. He could see only the crippled tank in the distance. One XM was missing.

The two behind kept pace. They had the best stabilizers of any tank ever built, but a man racing a motorcycle was a small and elusive target. The bad habits of Vietnam came out in their lavish expenditure of shells, ripping bare the earth all around Killy without killing the man. They didn't fire their missile, and Killy felt he knew why.

The missing XM had to have outflanked him, gone

ahead and hidden in one of the craters at the fence. They were herding him to it and he was helping them. So be it.

Killy drove with one hand and with his free arm pulled the TOW launcher off his shoulder. He was going at fifty over relatively flat ground. He tucked the launcher between his head and his shoulder. It was loaded. The eyepiece that controlled the missile through twin wires was shattered. All the missile carried was vegetable dye, but it was all he had.

From the craters ahead rose the malevolent silhouette of the missing XM. Its cannon jerked toward Killy. Killy let go of the handlebars completely to steady the launcher.

He fired first. The blast of the missile as it left the launcher almost knocked him off the bike, but he grabbed the bars with one hand. Twin wires sung out of the launcher tube as the missile rose and fell erratically over the ground. Killy continued to aim, hoping the sight control still functioned. The XM's machine guns fired, trying to knock the missile down.

Red paint exploded over the front of the tank. Without its warhead charge the missile had no more effect on the XM's armor than a BB. But the men inside were blind. Dye had gushed through the eye slits, covering men and controls with a gruesome coat of red. The tank lurched six inches forward and halted.

Killy dropped the launcher. The bike went from fifty to sixty. He rode straight at the blinded tank.

His weight back, he hit the lip of the crater and flew up. Then front wheel and back caromed off the XM's sloping turret. Killy threw his weight forward. Instead of flipping back, the Suzuki soared over the tank. At its apogee, the bike was fifteen feet in the air. It cleared the fence by five.

Killy landed on the rear wheel, brought down the front and never stopped. Abused, the Suzuki kept rattling on at thirty. Frustrated, the tanks were trapped on the moonscape of the firing range. In contrast, the war-game course looked positively pastoral to Killy. He swallowed and crossed himself.

World War III was coming to its conclusion on the game course. Men marked with red dye lay everywhere, smoking cigarettes. The few helicopters that were left droned aimlessly in the sky. Nobody paid any attention to Killy.

He worked his way back to the "friendly" command post. Trucks and tanks were parked in lines around the tent. There was a mood of self-congratulation, and Killy assumed that his side had won. He parked the battered motorcycle outside and gave it an affectionate tap. Then he went in.

The tent was crowded with officers, foreign and American. Cases of beer and ice had been broken open for the victors. There was a happy group around the triumphant computer and another, larger group around the map table. Pew and Jones were showing them how the last of the invading force had been driven back over its fictitious border.

"General Pew."

Pew looked up from his map. The gloat on his face shriveled as if he had seen a ghost. Killy wasn't far from it. His face and hands were bloody with lacerations from when he had fallen from the bike. Part of his pants was burned off. Jones was next to Pew. The colonel grabbed his pipe before it dropped out of his mouth.

You're dead, Jones's lips said without making a sound.

"General, I have a complaint," Killy stated.

It took Pew some time to find his voice.

"About what?"

"About the computer, sir. I think it set me down in the wrong place."

NINE

"WELL, IF YOU'RE not involved in this conspiracy, who are you?" Pew demanded. The three men, Pew, Jones and Killy, were in the general's office at Leavenworth. He'd decorated the room with the inevitable flags, photos of four-star friends and an artillery shell for a wastebasket.

"It would help if you told me what conspiracy," Killy said. He sat in Pew's easy chair. His burned fatigues had been replaced by the powder-blue uniform of the Swiss National Defense Force.

"You know damn well what."

"General, my name is Jean Mainz. I am a fellow officer and a guest. If you have any doubts, they'll be settled in the investigation."

"What investigation?" Pew asked Jones.

Jones had been present but silent, standing at a stiff "at ease" with his hands behind his back.

"He's already placed a phone call to the Swiss ambassador in Washington. He says he's going to make a formal protest," the colonel answered. "I think we might have made a mistake after all, General."

Pew frowned. He slumped into the chair behind his desk and chewed on a pencil, narrowing his eyes on Killy.

"Maybe you're that other agent, the one who was supposed to come and help us. Is that it?"

"Help us?" Jones raised an eyebrow.

Pew was irritated at the interruption, but he answered.

"Yes, there was some talk, very vague, about some outside agency picking up where Army Intelligence left off. Nobody said when he was going to turn up."

"Maybe you should have told us, sir." Jones squirmed with embarrassment. "Before we took this man out to kill him."

"The Army can take care of its own problems, Colonel," Pew reprimanded him. "We don't need help."

"All the computer said was that Mainz was agent material. It didn't say murder an ally." Jones spit the words out.

"That's enough, Colonel," Pew shouted. He stood up, his stomach in and chest and jaw out. Once again, Killy was struck by the immaculate perfection of the man, not only in his confidence-inspiring appearance but in the simplicity of his thought processes. An agent, any agent, among the officers was a slur on the Army. Kill the agent and you might kill an enemy. If it was the wrong agent, well, that wasn't too bad either.

Pew, in his majesty, turned to Killy.

"Colonel Mainz, are you an agent? If you are, I want you to know you will have our full cooperation."

"General," Killy replied, "I don't know what you're talking about."

"Then," Pew continued without a break, "I ask you

as an officer of a friendly nation to forget this incident and not make a protest. The damage to our nations' relations and to the General Staff and Command College would be enormous. I'm sure some sort of suitable commendation can be entered into your record here and I can assure you—" he glanced at Jones— "that the officers responsible for this outrage will be dealt with."

"I don't blame Colonel Jones. The orders didn't originate with him." Killy's eyes pinned Pew's in their sockets. "As a matter of fact, if any action is taken against him and not against the man who issued those orders, I will absolutely forward a protest to my embassy."

A flush spread over Pew's marble jaw. Killy waited till the general reached a good temperature before going on.

"However, I will take your word for it that you're fighting some sort of infiltration and that the attack on me was a mistake. And that disclosure of it would, at the very least, ruin the General Staff and Command College. I'd rather not be the cause of it, so I will suspend my protest. Suspend, not forget about it."

Killy gave the general no last psychological points. Without waiting to be dismissed, he put his hat on and went to the door.

"No more mistakes, General, not even by the computer."

In the midst of every great organization they rose. In the Vatican they were in the Curia bureaucracy, politicians in black who could quote statute or verse and had all the sympathy for man and understanding of God of a mole. They used to be in the Holy Office until the Illich Affair, and Cella was given the job of chasing them out. In the United States Army they were like Pew, uniformed images in love with themselves, building careers on phony body counts and a patriotism that sacrificed all for the good name of the Army and, incidentally, themselves.

Not a bad sermon, Killy congratulated himself. A gold star for Frank Killy.

Colonel Jones caught up with him as Killy reached the foreign-officers' quarters.

"Could I talk to you for a second?"

"Sure, you're still my sponsor."

Jones and Killy went into the recreation room. Except for two Japanese playing ping-pong at the far end, the room was empty. The television set was on, the sound off, the screen alive with Indians—American Indians—on horseback.

Jones stuck out his hand. "I want to apologize. I swear Pew never said a word about your investigation. The computer pointed you out as an agent. We knew the school was being infiltrated by agents among the foreign students, so . . ."

Killy accepted the handshake. Some of the chagrin went out of Jones's face.

"I also want to thank you for not letting the prick railroad me. Up to then, I never really knew him. I mean, I'd served under him in Vietnam and I didn't know." Jones shrugged. "Here I am crying on the shoulder of someone I tried to put underground. Anyway, thanks."

"You're welcome. But I want to get one thing clear. I'm nothing but Colonel Jean Mainz. I'm not an agent and I know nothing about infiltrations or plots."

His apologies over, the black colonel regarded Killy

more objectively. A smile grew despite his rue. He started to speak when Killy abruptly went to the television and turned up the sound. War whoops poured out of the speaker. Jones had anticipated the move. Any surveillance bug would be foiled by the howling of Hollywood extras.

Jones picked up when Killy returned. "I was saying, that no one was going to bother you again, Colonel Mainz. I also wanted to add that if you were investigating what's been happening here, if, as a matter of fact, you were an agent, that you did the right thing not letting the general know."

That was something Killy had decided long ago. He said nothing.

"Okay." Jones shook his head. "You're just a little Swiss colonel who ruined two million dollars' worth of XM tanks, and we should trade the computer for a Coke machine. I don't blame you. Good luck."

Killy watched the colonel go and then went himself up to his room. Malik was in it, relaxing in front of a *Playboy* centerfold.

"I've discovered something important today," the Indonesian confided. "Something they want to keep secret from all the foreign officers."

Killy dropped on his bed. He crossed his ankles, just enough to irritate their second-degree burns, and uncrossed them.

"Aspirin?"

"Bunnies," Malik said.

The two officers looked at each other, mutually confused.

"Do you have any aspirin?" Killy asked.

Comprehension hit Malik's face. He dug into his kit

and threw Killy a tin of aspirins.

The secret agent's secret weapon, Killy thought, and tossed two pills down his throat.

"Bunnies," Malik repeated with greater emphasis. "General Pew never mentioned them. It says in here there is a Playboy Club in Kansas City. And they call them *Bunnies!*"

Killy had never heard a word pronounced so erotically in his life. Malik seemed to be in the middle of a religious experience.

"Do you want to be alone by any chance?" Killy asked.

Malik didn't hear him. "There are no better lovers than the women of Bali. Eager. Intuitive. Very skilled. It's said they practice with monkeys. I don't know for a fact. But to have a Bunny. We have to rent a car."

"Why not a Honda?"

Malik still wasn't listening.

"They even have bunny ears!"

The reverie was broken by a messenger at the door. He gave Killy a sealed folder from Colonel Jones.

Killy broke the folder open in the bathroom. Inside was an envelope with the title: TRICAP Study Material. Inside the envelope were complete computer printouts of the security checks on every instructor in the college, including Jones and up to Pew. Killy stuffed the contents back in the folder.

"Kansas City?" Malik chirped as Killy left the bathroom.

"An ear man. I don't think I've ever met one of those before. To each his own."

"Where are you going?"

"You've got me all excited. I'm going to go listen to some classical music and have an orgy."

The war college had soundproofed booths where foreign officers improved their English with language records. When school was not in session, the officers were allowed to play records from the school's music library. Killy chose Prokofiev's *Lieutenant Kije* suite.

As the record began, he opened the folder again. Jones and MASSTER were as complete as he could have wished. Every instructor was analyzed by family background, sexual habits, credit rating, bank statements and career data. Where the computer's data wasn't thorough, Jones had written marginal comments. One officer drank heavily but had dried out recently. Another was an addict, the result of heavy morphine injections for war wounds. The other officers controlled his drug use.

The background music was especially appropriate for Pew. Lieutenant Kije, the Russian story went, was a fictitious officer created by courtiers to cheer up a czar when his armies were doing badly in the field. Where other officers ran, Kije stood and fought. When others cursed the czar, Kije prayed for him. In return, the czar sent decoration after decoration to the nonexistent hero. At last, the czar wanted to see his model officer and summoned him to court. The courtiers were thrown into confusion, until one hit on the logical solution. Kije, overjoyed by the czar's invitation, fights even more valiantly and dies in battle. The last movement of the suite ends in a flourish of trumpets.

Pew's career was cardboard. He was a rear-echelon general who faked combat flying time, exaggerated body counts and kissed every ass in the Pentagon. The problem was that, in his way, Pew was still loyal. He'd no sooner betray the war college than let his hair grow to the stars on his shoulders.

Pew was a disease, but he wasn't the disease that destroyed Naherman, Hamid, Novick and DeBeer. None of the instructors was.

Killy returned the folder to Colonel Jones's office. Colonel Hilliard was sitting at Jones's desk.

"Colonel Jones sent this to me. He must have meant it for someone else."

As Hilliard put the folder in a drawer, Killy saw a streak of red dye on the colonel's wrist. The dye must have exploded into the tank with enough force to impregnate the skin.

"Anything else you want me to tell him?" Hilliard asked.

"No, thanks, you've been enough help."

On his way back to Malik and his magazines, Killy stopped in Jones's classroom. It was deserted. He picked up a piece of chalk and wrote on the blackboard: *Students?*

Then he continued on to his quarters, whistling first Prokofiev and next, in honor of his roommate, the "Kansas City Blues."

TEN

JONES DELIVERED security reports on all the college students, American and foreign. It took Killy a day to study them because a number of the government reports on foreign students were scanty. The French took a particular delight in saying as little as possible about the officers they were sending. English security reports were complete, but English security was lousy. In the end it didn't matter. Killy agreed with Jones that there wasn't one possible infiltrator in all the rest of the class.

Malik was the least possible. Killy's roommate had followed through with his promise to lease a car for the duration of the college. It was a red Corvette. Paradoxically, the more time Malik put in driving his car back and forth to Kansas City, the better his studies went.

"It's simple. In everything I do, I must be inspired first. It's the Indonesian personality. To make love without guilt, for unrestrained pleasure, I must have my work out of the way. I've seen more than one man have his love-making powers decreased by niggling concerns about family or work."

Things like that would niggle, Killy agreed. Cella had the best answer to the problem. An Inquisitor was chosen for his lack of family. Killy's relatives were Boston Irish. When he came out of the Army to go into Harvard, he thought they'd be proud. They were, but they were also distant. He'd become different, out of their ken, somehow dangerous to them. Killy wasn't married, and as long as he remained an Inquisitor, and therefore a lay brother, he had to remain single. Every job had a silver lining.

As for guilt about not doing a job right, that was a luxury no Inquisitor knew. If you didn't do it right, you were dead. Now that, Killy felt, was inspiration.

Only he wasn't doing the job. Four men tried to shake the world. They were officers from different countries who happened to attend one American war college. In place of mystery, Killy had found coincidence. More bored than upset, he asked Malik's permission to take the Corvette out for a drive.

"What for? You have no vices to pursue," the roommate said as he gave Killy the keys.

"Maybe I can find some."

The Corvette had a speedometer that reached 150. The limit on Kansas highways was 80. Killy compromised between the two and cruised over the flat landscape. Billboards announcing the Second Coming and the latest in tractors flashed by. Crows and chicken hawks dotted the sky.

Don't let them get you too, the Drobski girl had said. That was his only clue. Who was "them"?

A hundred miles away from Leavenworth, Killy became hungry and pulled off at a diner. There were truck drivers at the long aluminum-and-formica counter and at a corner booth was Mrs. Cero. There was no mistaking her amused green eyes, hair as black as his but finer and a beauty that made Killy's stomach tighten.

"What is a Swiss colonel doing in a place like this?" she asked as he sat down in the booth.

"Going native."

She had a light summer dress, light enough for him to notice that her breasts were slightly larger than Caterina's.

"What should I try?" he asked.

She had a plate of apple pie and coffee. Only one bite was gone from the pie and her fork lay on the edge of the dish like something forlorn. Killy went back to his examination of Mrs. Cero. Malik's talk of Bunnies had left an echo in Killy.

"The coffee won't kill you," she said.

"That's comforting."

"Yeah?" a nasal voice asked over his shoulder. He turned to face the dreariest waitress in Kansas. Her white uniform was smeared with catsup and her blond hair was underlined by dark roots.

"Coffee and a double hamburger, rare."

"You want a side order of potato chips?"

"Fine."

The waitress studied his Swiss uniform.

"Are you a cop?"

"No."

"Good. If you were a cop you could eat free."

She left, feeling she had outwitted him.

"A hamburger rare," Mrs. Cero commented. "You pick up American things fast."

"I'd like to. My name is Jean. What is yours?"

"Marie. Oh, come on, Colonel—Jean—you're not going to tell me how lonely it is for a foreign officer in a strange country and how you'd just like some understanding companionship?"

"No. At least not until after we went to bed."

When the waitress came back with the double hamburger, rare, the booth was empty. A five-dollar tip lay on the table.

"Snobs," she muttered and tucked the bill in her bra.

Killy and Marie Cero found a motel ten miles up the road. She stayed in her car while he signed in, using the name Romagno. For another twenty dollars the clerk sold him a bottle of gin and a bag of ice. Their cabin was made of masonite with a thin, rosewood veneer. The bureau was stained pine and the television set got one station, but the sheets were clean, the mattress was firm, and there was a bathroom. If a tornado appeared, the whole motel would be picked up like a matchbox. It was a chance Killy was willing to take.

Marie came naked out of the bathroom. She'd let her black hair down and it reached to the middle of her back. She had a slim waist and her thighs were more muscled than he expected, pleasantly muscled and accentuating her smallish, round buttocks. Her breasts were large without falling into lushness, their caps small and dark. The tip of her abdomen was marked by a triangle of brown curls, so neat it might have been trimmed.

Killy was still in his pants. She unbuckled his belt and slid her hands inside, feeling his size as she kissed his mouth.

"Maybe it's been a long time for you, but its been longer for me," she said without coyness.

He stepped out of the last of his clothes and carried her to the bed.

"I thought your husband could cure any problem."

"Let's not talk about him."

She slid her leg over his, letting him rise up between her thighs. The lips of her sex spread and let him in. As he filled her, Marie held onto his face, staring in his eyes. Her eyelids closed, and a shudder went through her hips as he pulled her buttocks into him and rolled them in a slow circle.

Marie had two orgasms the first time and three the second. By then it was late afternoon. Half the gin was gone and the ice was melted but neither was drunk, even high. Sex had burned up the alcohol.

She lay with her head resting on his stomach, smoking a cigarette. Absent-mindedly, he stroked her breasts.

"It's the man that's supposed to smoke afterwards in America, isn't it?" she asked.

"I don't know. You'll have to tell me."

"You know, it was just because we happened to meet that I did this. But—" she cupped his hand on her breast—"it was worth it. No emotion and no lying, just two people who wanted to have each other." She rolled her eyes to meet his, her face as calm as a madonna again. "You were good, Jean."

"Were? Never again?"

She sat up, relaxed and satisfied, her breasts hanging just a little. For some reason, they excited him again because of it.

"I am not faithful to Kelton. He's a bad lover, and perhaps I've made a bad bargain in marrying him. Sex is important to me."

Killy knew. He was drained.

"But I won't ruin him with a scandal," she added. "If the opportunity rises to make love with someone as handsome and charming and talented as you, I'll take it. But that's all, my dear Jean."

The cheap curtains mellowed the sun. A golden light covered her fair skin. She smiled.

"All right, we're well suited," she said. "You like me in bed and I like you. Now, I've got a long drive ahead of me and so have you."

She jumped up and went into the bathroom. Killy heard the sound of a shower and, despite the small size of the shower stall, joined her. When they stepped out of the stall to dry themselves, they made love again, standing up, Marie's back pressed into the tile wall.

"We'll have to arrange something," she gasped at the end.

Two days later, Killy rented his own car and drove to another motel sixty miles from Leavenworth. Marie was waiting for him. She was waiting again a week later in a Wichita hotel lobby when he arrived.

Killy found her the perfect partner: bright, casual and, in bed, imaginative and tireless. Marie didn't mention her husband and didn't ask about Leavenworth. All she demanded was sex, and Killy was hedonist enough to provide it. There were times when she struck him as cold and he recoiled, but all the time their sexual attachment grew.

At Leavenworth, he carried on his investigation with Jones's covert help. The tension was gone, though. He was sure whatever happened to the dead officers didn't happen at the school. On Killy's request, Jones provided the security clearance papers on Drobski.

Drobski had cheated at the University of Kansas and bribed his way to becoming president of his fraternity house. During the Second World War, he was ineligible for the draft because he had a farmer's status and was thus vital to the war effort. Drobski used his time wisely, buying up small farms that couldn't compete with the low monopoly prices at which he sold his wheat, soy beans, peas, corn and sorghum to the Army. Once the war was over, he joined the National Guard and Civil Defense, meeting more politicians in each and using his influence to become a reserve officer and sell unproductive land to the U.S. Army Corps of Engineers at inflated prices. Under cover of his Committee to Preserve Rural Virtues, he lobbied for Drobski interests with other people's money. Drobski's savings and loan associations had on their boards the state senators whose job it was to regulate Drobski's real-estate speculations. Only when some tax loopholes were closed did Drobski begin taking tax losses by establishing foundations such as the Carla Drobski Center For Psychotherapy. While the Center was near the campus of his alma mater, it had no association with it, and its director, Dr. Cero, was unknown in medical circles. Drobski had hidden money in Mexican ranches, "sweetheart" farm union pension funds, and in the Credit Suisse in Geneva.

Altogether, Harvey Drobski was a successful, go-getting businessman, a good family man, and innocent of any conspiracy to undermine the security of the United States.

Killy kept attending classes and, when the rest of the officers were going off to art galleries and factory tours, meeting Marie. There were worse ways to run an Inquisition.

ELEVEN

MARIE SHIFTED her weight. Her buttocks fit into his hips and she began rocking on all fours, against each thrust. The harder she rocked the more her breasts swayed. His hands went from the small of her back to her hips, tilting them up so he could drive deeper from behind. She clamped her thighs shut and held him inside, her sex squeezing the last of his climax. Instead of crying out, she bit her hand and a deep blush spread from her face and over her breasts and back.

Killy rolled off onto the rug. He picked a pubic curl off his penis.

Marie remained face down on the carpet. It was Persian, maroon with dark blue designs. She seemed fragile and white on it, a nineteenth-century Romanticist's erotic dream. It made him wonder. It was her house. They were using it while Cero was off at some convention. Did Kelton Cero choose the rug?

She raised her head and looked through her disheveled hair at him.

"I'm beat. No, I know I like it every way but I'm not

a masochist. I just mean I'm tired. It'll be nice, you sleeping overnight. What excuse did you give?"

"I am visiting relatives in Chicago."

"Good. We can pretend incest next." She laughed. She got half up and walked on her knees to the coffee table. "I'm afraid we have nothing but brandy."

"I'll pretend I'm Napoleon."

"Good."

Still on her knees, she brought him a snifter an inch deep in brandy. She knelt to watch him drink.

"Aren't you going to have any?"

"I hate the stuff," she said. "I think Kelton buys it out of spite. Now, I'm going to put something on. I may be an adultress, but I'm no nudist."

She got to her feet and ran up the stairs to the bedroom. Killy was left alone in the living room. He finished the brandy and walked around, looking at bindings in the bookcases. They were what he might have expected. Medical tomes and book-club selections. For a confidence man, Cero had surprisingly Middle American tastes.

On the wall was a photo of the Ceros with Drobski and family. Carlotta looked even more miserable than usual in it. Killy strolled over to the desk. On its leather top was a picture of Marie. The top drawer was locked.

He heard Marie whistling from the second floor. Killy pulled his pants on. He took his wallet out and removed the plastic identification card all Leavenworth personnel had to carry. He slid it through the top of the drawer and pressed down. The drawer jerked open into his hands.

There was nothing inside but a black Moroccan notebook. The first heading was under the letter N, and there were notations in a woman's hand of motels and dates. The second heading was *DB*. There were more motels and dates. There were three more headings, *Na, H* and *M*. He didn't have to look to know the motel listings under *M* were correct.

Novick, DeBeer, Naherman and Hamid. And Mainz. Army security hadn't been able to track them because they'd done the same thing he did, hid their own tracks for the most common, human reason of all: a woman. Marie just had to lie in bed while they hid the trail. The same way he did. Carlotta, in her simple, confused way, was right. Marie got them all.

"Naughty Jean. Reading other people's diaries."

Marie had come down the steps without him hearing. She had changed into a surgical gown. In her hand was a revolver.

Why hadn't he heard her? Killy looked at the empty glass of brandy. He took a step toward her, and his right leg splayed over the floor.

He tried to talk. His tongue felt swollen and his lips were numb. He held onto the desk chair and it fell on the floor. He fell after it, rolling woodenly over and over. One eye was dug into the carpet. With the other, he saw the door to the living room open.

Cero entered with two assistants. Like Marie, they were dressed in surgical gowns.

Killy's eyes unfocused, looking in opposite directions. He felt a tongue depressor being shoved into his mouth so he wouldn't swallow it.

"Colonel Mainz? Colonel Mainz, can you hear me?"

Cero was looking down at him. The ceiling was different, bare beams. He had been out and they'd moved him to the cellar. He wondered how long he'd been unconscious.

"Don't try to talk. You can't. Don't worry, you're

responding well. You have a strong constitution."

That's nice to know, Killy thought. But what the hell is going on?

"The drug was only so that we could give you an injection. The injection was only to keep you from harming yourself. We are your friends."

The vagueness was gone from Kelton Cero's face. In its place was purpose and amiable confidence.

"You can't move your head or any part of your body; however, your involuntary functions are proceeding. There is no danger of suffocation. You are just experiencing a temporary deadening of the lower brain stem. I'm sorry we have to use these measures, but you are expected back at the command school on Monday, and we have so little time."

Marie's head moved into view. "How is he?"

"Fine. Look at his pupils. He's taking in every word."

Her face loomed down at Killy. It had exactly the concern she would have shown for a laboratory rat. When she looked at her husband, her face was transformed by admiration.

"I don't know how they train you in Switzerland in the resistance of so-called brainwashing techniques," Cero said, smiling paternally. "I just want to assure you that resistance won't help. Let me put it this way: You won't resist. Other techniques—physical torture, psychological torture—are basically the same. That is, they work from the outside in. I reverse the method."

Experimentally, Killy tried to move a finger, then realized he couldn't see it move if it did. He tried slowing his heart. He could feel that pulsing away at the same rate.

"I explain the method to you because it will diminish the terror. Terror slows us. I don't think we'll have as great a problem with you because you seem to know something about the brain."

Suddenly Cero's face was blocked from view. Killy was looking at a photograph. It was an X ray of a skull. Traveling around inside it were a dozen tiny wires.

"Electrodes," Cero's voice explained. "This is the brain of an epileptic. The electrodes can be used for two purposes: to destroy abnormal brain tissue, or to stimulate brain tissue in the pleasure center or septal region of the brain. Even now, epileptics are walking around with these electrodes implanted in their brain. You are no epileptic, but all animals share some things in common: pleasure centers and pain centers. Before patriotism or treason, before courage or cowardice come these centers. In the frontal lobes, we find man's reasoning power is almost an afterthought of the limbic system deep in his brain. That is where the septal region and his pain centers are located. Stimulate a pleasure center—" Cero oozed ecstasy—"and an animal feels something that makes sex pitiful. Monkeys fitted with electrodes there spend their entire lives pressing a button that shoots euphoria throughout their bodies. Stimulate a pain center. . . ."

Killy's mind split in two. He tried to scream, but his face was frozen. The cells of his brain seemed to be disintegrating, as if a rat had borrowed through his skull and was eating it, grasping and tearing out the gray-pink pulp. Then it was gone. The table Killy was lying on was slick with his sweat and his eyes teared.

"His heart beat really went up that time," a male voice said.

"Of course," Cero answered. "That, Colonel Mainz, was a pain center. Stimulate that and a cat will kill itself trying to escape a mouse, or a man will follow orders. I think you are beginning to understand. Or perhaps you think I'm being a sadist."

Waves of pleasure rolled through Killy. The table was a cloud. He was weightless, calm and peaceful. He loved Cero, loved everyone. He lay on top of the universe. These people were his friends.

His vision cleared. It was the same Cero.

"See? It all depends on you whether we stimulate one center or the other. Naturally, we can't have you walking around with electrodes when you leave here. My modest contribution to this research has been the substitution of low-pulse lasers for electrodes. You may know that high-pulse lasers are used regularly for knifeless surgery, including the destruction of abnormal brain tissue. I don't want to destroy your brain, only use it. The low-pulse laser will leave no lasting damage, let me assure you. You will be a stimulated animal with set patterns, but isn't that what you are now? Only your stimulation has been the lower stimulation of sex, and your pattern was set around an available woman."

Killy's pupils dilated. He could do nothing else. Cero's head moved away. Other preparations were taking place. Killy became aware of restraining straps being fastened around his arms and legs. A collar snapped shut around his throat. He felt a strap over his chest and a harness around his head. He could smell coffee. With a lot of effort, he could make a noise in his throat.

"The injection is wearing off." Cero's face reappeared. "Try to talk."

Killy's tongue returned to normal size and felt along the smooth sides of his teeth. He felt his hand when he made a fist.

"Talk," Cero ordered.

"Screw yourself," Killy said in German.

At once, his body was snapping like a bow against the straps. An inhuman scream filled the basement. Muscles jerked in spasms against each other. Killy couldn't stop screaming to breathe. His face began turning blue.

The pain went. Killy sank, beaten, on the table. Air rushed in through the spittle of his lips.

"We have to break these bad habits in the beginning," Cero explained. "And we will convince you. Your own body will persuade you."

As Cero explained, Killy desperately thought. He knew how to counter interrogation. If the questioner applied friendliness, respond with friendliness, overwhelm him with trust and half-truths. If he applied physical pain and disfigurement, the mind had to divorce itself from the body, to look at a mutilated hand as an accident in another country. Killy had had battery charges run through his testicles, his hands burned with an acetylene torch, spent months in solitary confinement. This was different. This time he had no more control over his mind than a runaway car. His brain, his one true defense, had turned traitor.

"We will know whether your answers are truthful or not. For your health, we are reading your respiration rate, heartbeat and perspiration loss. It so happens that they are the elements of a polygraph machine, or lie detector."

Muscular contractions could confuse a polygraph. Did Cero know that? Killy wondered.

"Don't flex your feet when you answer," Cero said, as if he could read Killy's mind. "Your shoes are off and we'll see you doing it. The mirror?" he asked someone else.

An overhead mirror was swung over Killy's chest and its angle set so that he was looking directly at his head. Cero said nothing; nothing needed to be said.

A leather and steel harness ran over his forehead and around his jaws, making his black hair stand up like a bush. In the middle of his hair, like a garish crest, were four ruby-red Laser tubes, the tip of each tube pressed into his skull and locked in place by wires runing from the harness.

Killy thought the picture was familiar and he remembered why. He had seen the same helpless expression on too many laboratory monkeys.

"My name is Colonel Jean. . . ."

He didn't finish. The face in the mirror contorted in agony. Blood ran from its mouth as he bit himself. The first tube glowed, a cathode tube defining and redefining light, turning light into a concentrated beam that poured through his skull deep into his brain—into the seat of nightmares and animal horror.

Pain ended. Killy sobbed.

"We'll try it again," Cero said. Killy heard the sound of a match being struck and the inhalation of a cigarette.

"Jean . . ."

Pain. End of pain. Killy couldn't think. His brain was gutted, hollow.

"Jean . . ."

Pain, end of pain. The flick of a switch. The lie, the pain. Again and again.

"You are a remarkable specimen," Cero said to Killy and winked at Marie.

"I am Je—"

Cero let the laser flow, closing his ears to Killy's screams. The assistant watching the heartbeat accelerate like a rocket waved his arm. Cero turned the pain off. Killy continued to shake with spasms, his body's protest.

The Swiss was just as likely to go mad rather than break. Either that or have his heart stop. Then Cero would have to start all over with another candidate. The doctor switched tactics.

"How many feet do you have?" he asked Killy. "How many?"

He leaned over to hear. Killy's lips trembled with fear, hardly daring to whisper.

"Two."

Warmth and pleasure filled his body. His brain glowed, basking in the laser's ray. Just as he had no control over the terror, Killy couldn't hold back the orgasms of well-being and trust. They poured out of the core of his brain, overpowering the reasoning frontal lobe, making personality and resistance melt. His eyes and lips were closed in ecstasy.

"Very good. What color is your hair?"

"Black."

The reward flowed through him again. He sighed. The individual disappeared. All that was left were twelve billion nerve cells transmitting and receiving, starting at the limbic system, the gratifying, all-encompassing pulse of light. From paleocortex to neocortex, down the long nerve threads of the spinal column and outward to the skin the ripples flowed.

The flow stopped.

"What is your name?"

Marie asked it. Her face hovered over him. She was

more beautiful than ever, a Renaissance virgin. The lasers hummed in anticipation. Killy hung between their heaven and hell.

There was no hesitation in his answer.

"Francis Xavier Killy."

TWELVE

"This is a bonus," Cero exulted. "We were just hoping for a Swiss officer who could help us to some gold bullion. We never even knew the Holy office existed. But an Inquisitor, a bodyguard of the Pope himself is much more helpful."

It was Saturday morning. Killy had been brought from his cell and, too sedated to offer resistance, been strapped again to the table.

"You killed the Army investigator. How can I help you?"

"The other investigator was just an investigator. But you are something else."

Cero waited for reactions of hostility. Killy remained as placid as a lab monkey, the harness clamped on his temples.

"Good," the doctor continued. "After a difficult start, perfect progress."

"Be careful." Marie approached the table. "I've been monitoring the readings. He doesn't believe you."

Killy let no surprise show on his face. Marie was

right. During his few unsedated moments he had worked out their method. Cero's claims had to be lies because laser research was expensive, more expensive than even Drobski's donations could cover. It needed cathode ray tubes, rubies to define light, and powerful generators to produce the light. Cero was still a charlatan.

"My wife, who knows you well, says that the reasoning lobe of your brain still hopes for some miracle. If you have some questions, please ask them," Cero opened his hands. He might have been a lecturer in front of a college class.

Killy answered like a bright student.

"Drugs. You've been drugging me from the start. During our 'session' you never let me see my hand. For all I know you have a tube in my wrist."

"And what would we give you through the tube?"

"Dopamine. Norepinephrine. Either one would create the reactions I've been having."

Cero smiled and at that instant Killy knew he was wrong. It was not a charlatan's bluff.

"An excellent defense fantasy. You'll see your arms."

Killy felt fingers on the buckles at his wrists. Tentatively, he raised his arms. There were rings of bruised flesh at the elbows and wrists, but there were no puncture marks anywhere.

"You put the tube in me someplace else."

"You need another demonstration."

"That won't convince me."

"Another kind of demonstration."

The lasers glowed, making Killy jump. But there was no pain or sensation of pleasure. Cero was using the two rear lasers this time. Marie smiled with her old amusement.

Cero removed a pen and a pencil from the pocket of his surgical smock. The pen he placed in Killy's right hand and the pencil in his left.

"What's the idea?" Killy asked.

"Very simple," Cero replied. "Just tell me what you're holding in your right hand."

"A pen." Cero's question seemed stupid.

"And now, Mr. Killy, what is in your left?"

Killy stared at the pencil. No word came to his mind. He turned it over. There was still no word.

"What are you holding in your left hand? Haven't you ever seen one before?"

A different kind of terror brought the sweat out on Killy's face. He could see the pencil clearly. He felt no pain. His brain simply refused to work.

"In your right hand?"

"A pen, damn it."

"Your left?"

"A . . ."

Killy turned the pencil over faster and faster. What was it? He blinked the sweat out of his eyes. The Ceros and their two assistants stood over him, waiting for an answer they knew couldn't come. He squeezed the pencil in his hand. Wood and lead snapped in two.

"I have more *pencils*," Cero remarked. "A *pencil*, Mr. Killy."

Killy lay in his damp harness. Cero put a tongue depressor in Killy's left hand. Killy's mouth garbled words that meant nothing. Finally, he let it drop to the floor. He could smell the fear emanating from his pores.

"No drugs," Cero explained. "The lasers are intercepting the corpus callosum, the connection between the right hemisphere of your brain and the left hemisphere. In right-handed persons, the speech area of the

brain is in the left hemisphere. You can name the pen
in your right hand because its sensory message goes
directly to the left hemisphere. The message from your
left hand goes to the right hemisphere, and as the right
hemisphere is no longer communicating with the other
hemisphere, you are, shall we say, struck dumb."

"A trick."

"Would you care to see another? You still have the
pen in your right hand. Take it apart."

Killy grasped the pen in both hands. He began un-
screwing the top with his right hand. His left hand
screwed it back. He tried to work faster. His right unscrewed and the left screwed. It was out of control
with a life of its own. No, with a life directed by the
half of his brain he had lost to Cero. His fingers
worked frantically, until the pen flew out of his war-
ring hands.

The hum stopped. His hand had been returned to
him. Killy lay still as the assistants toweled the sweat
from him.

Four men had gone before him, and four men had
been broken. Their brains had been split in two and
twisted like dough. The penalty for adultery was rising.
The penalty for stupidity was the same, though. He
should have known the passionate Marie wanted more
than a warm body. Cella would be disappointed.
Romagno would say he told everyone so.

On his closed lids, Killy saw Marie turning in bed
to him. Her hand was on his, bringing it to her body,
placing it on her hip.

"Here," she said.

He had no trouble naming the object in his hand. It
was a gun. Running from the grip was an electrical
cord. She swung the mirror over his head.

"The gun has a photoelectric beam," she said. "When the beam hits the mirror it will turn off the laser."

The lights were turned off, all except for a light coming from the side and hitting the mirror.

"More tricks?" Killy asked tonelessly.

"Oh, the games are over," Cero said from behind him. "This is strictly business."

The room went entirely black. He heard the click of a slide projector.

There was a logical progession in Cero's method, Killy thought, from taking control of the brain, to splitting the brain, to. . . . Only no brain was left.

The image of a face swam up over the mirror. Killy didn't have time to recognize it before the pain seized his skull. It was more intense than ever, making his eyes burn in their sockets.

"Shoot!" Cero yelled.

His skull was about to explode. His arm jerked up. Killy wasn't directing it; he was a spectator to himself. His finger squeezed the trigger and shot the face.

Soothing pleasure rewarded him. He stopped shaking.

The face appeared again and with it the pain. Killy's hand was quicker. The beam turned agony to luxurious comfort. His eyes and gun waited tensely for the face to show itself again. It did. Pain, shot, reward. Ten times, twenty times, a hundred times. When the lights went back on, they had to peel the gun from his hands.

"I got him, didn't I?" Killy asked eagerly.

"You did very well," Cero reassured him.

The assistants helped Killy back to his cell. For the first time, he was given solid food. It wasn't until he finished the meal that he realized that, over and over, he had shot the Pope.

The food choked in his throat.

"No!"

He threw the tray against the walls. The assistants came in and threw him on the floor. A needle sank into his arm.

The skull harness was mobile. They trussed him into it and put the gun on the far side of the basement. When the face was flashed onto a wall and the pain began, he had to run across the room, pick up the gun and fire.

He swore he wouldn't the first time, but he did. The second time he tried throwing himself against a wall and smashing the tubes. He no sooner started when the pain increased and he collapsed futilely. He crawled to the gun and fired again and again until the face vanished and pleasure pulsed through his nerves.

"You see what a simple method it is." Cero beamed. "No password is necessary, no plan to fall apart. All we need is a conditioned man. We set the pattern in your brain—the face, the need to avoid pain, the shot —and we have the perfect assassin. Of course, with a hardy specimen like you we will have to make sure the pattern is set."

They took precautions to keep their assassin. Marie opened the door that led from the basement.

"Escape," she said.

The Ceros and their assistants stood at the other end of the room. Killy staggered to the door. He reached it when the pain drove him to his knees.

"Escape!" Cero shouted.

Killy stirred and the pain overwhelmed him again. In the end he dragged himself back to the Ceros. A reward of pleasure welcomed him. Marie patted his cheek.

"Rest now," she said.

Back in his cell, Killy tried to think. The very concept of trying the cell door brought on a headache. He fell asleep. A dream came of him walking into St. Peter's Basilica. The church was filled with worshippers. A small man in rich vestments performed Mass beneath the great altar canopy. Killy felt at peace with the congregation. The small man turned with the chalice and hosts. It was the Holy Father.

Killy woke up, shaking and sweating. His arm was held out rigidly and his index finger moved back and forth as if it were shooting every bullet in a gun.

Jesus, how am I going to get out of this, he wondered, besides a goddam miracle?

His head sank against the cell wall. It was padded and covered with a gray plastic material to keep him from harming himself. Better accommodations than his dungeon under the Vatican.

Hail Mary, Mother of God, pray for us sinners now and in the hour of our death. Or our transformation from lecherous fool to a conditioned brain.

He repeated the formula over and over.

Through the night, he was fitted with the skull harness again. The gun was put in a bureau of five drawers. When the image of His Holiness erupted painfully on a wall, Killy had to cross the room and find the gun before firing.

"That's odd. His dexterity is improving. This is usually their worst stage," Marie noted.

"We never had an Inquisitor to work with before," Cero said proudly.

Hail Mary, Killy repeated in the corner of his brain

that remained his own. He'd already repeated it a thousand times when they took him back to his cell.

Sunday was the last day of conditioning. Killy was strapped on the table, the gun in his hand.

"Your assignment is in two parts. You will fire twice," Cero instructed him.

The face emerged on the mirror. Killy fired. The lights went on. He stared at his own reflection. He struggled against the searing pain. His hand jerked up.

"Fire," Marie whispered.

Killy fired. Soft comfort flooded his mind. Now he knew what his reward was: death.

The patterning lasted for hours. Kill the Pope, kill himself. Assassinate and suicide, operation and clean-up all in one. Hail the limbic system, ruler of the cortex.

"You'll return to the command school tomorrow. Before you go, we'll erase your memory of everything that happened here. You will operate as normally as usual, return to your post in Rome and, when your new pattern is triggered, complete your mission." Cero rubbed his hands. "You'll have to excuse me if I'm feeling pleased with myself. If this method works on someone like you, you see, it will work on anyone."

"Even you?"

"On anything with a nervous system." He put his hand, with an executioner's false affection, on Killy's shoulder. "Between the two of us we will upset the world."

"Why? Why kill him?"

Cero smirked, the beard spreading around his lips.

"Another man would have asked why the suicide was necessary. Since you didn't, I'll answer you. I could say it was because of the money that can be made with advance information about catastrophes of this kind. You can imagine what will happen to Italian and American stocks. But the truth is, I am doing it because it can be done."

Killy was dragged to his cell for the night. His own mind was the real cell, a landmined ring around potential rebellion. Was that what Cero was after, what he was trying to prove, his superiority to the Church? A better hell?

"Through me the way to the woeful city," Dante read on his gates to hell, "through me the way to eternal pain. Abandon all hope, ye that enter."

Cero waited in the Inferno with a scalpel and a laser.

Hail Mary, Killy began. It was his hope, no matter whether he believed in it or not. Anything to keep from total disintegration. The first Hail Mary he'd said when he was four. Up to the age of sixteen, he must have said ten thousand of them. Since he became an Inquisitor, he'd probably said twenty thousand more. Could the lasers burn out a brain pattern as deep as that?

Pray for us sinners now and in the hour of our death.

THIRTEEN

"BREAKFAST," the assistant announced as he came into the cell. His smile was decorated by a steel tooth.

Killy was sitting on his bunk. As the assistant put the tray down, Killy grabbed the lapels of the man's smock and rolled back. The assistant was still accelerating when his head hit the wall. Killy dumped him unconscious on the floor and searched for a gun. There wasn't one; Cero was that confident. The Inquisitor faced the open door.

A headache rose from nowhere. With each step to the door it grew, as if a force field blocked the way out. Killy held his eyes shut and felt his way.

Hail Mary, Mother of God.

The pain increased, not the pain of the laser but the reaction of his body to the threat of the glowing tube. His stomach rose to his mouth and his legs locked, unwilling to take the final step out of the cell. Killy swayed and pitched forward, landing in the hall.

Pray for us sinners.

The pain subsided, but only partially. He could

walk by supporting himself on the wall. Killy dragged himself up the basement stairs and pushed the door at the top of the steps open with his head.

He could see across the living-room floor to a foyer and the front door. It was open, forming a rectangle of sunlight and a normal American street. He crawled into the living room and hoisted himself by a chair to his feet.

Squinting, repeating the Hail Mary, Killy started for the door. The light danced as he stumbled toward it, but it grew. He was out of the living room and in the foyer. He could hear birds and cars.

"He's escaping!"

Marie was halfway down the stairs from the second floor. She was incredulous, amazed, and she didn't have a gun. Killy was only feet from the door.

The light was blocked by a man's silhouette. One of the assistants had been on the porch the whole time. He was as surprised as Marie, but he recovered, closing the door behind him and drawing a club from his smock.

Killy swung, but his fist was pitifully slow and missed by six inches. The assistant merely stepped back and brought his club down, once, twice, three times. The Ceros' fifth experiment collapsed on the floor.

Death wasn't a cushion of pleasure, Killy discovered, and Hail Marys didn't produce angel voices. As he always suspected, death was a coffin.

The coffin shook and rolled him from side to side. Metal angles dug into his back and legs. For a corpse it was very irritating. His headache was the usual kind a club on the head could produce. The Ceros, he had the feeling, were nowhere near.

He felt for where a lid should have been. There was only more curved metal. Wind whistled through the coffin's seams. He found a latch on the side and pulled it open.

Killy looked out a glass panel and drew back. Outside the panel was five thousand feet of open sky. Light poured in on the stenciled letters inside the glass: RIGHT FUSELAGE PANEL D-2 DRONE PROP USAF. An arrow showed which end was up.

"Son of a bitch."

He knew enough about drones to know they were nothing but flying tubes. Sometimes they were towed. This one wasn't; he could feel the jet engine behind a panel at his feet. Their controls could be set for level flight by an automatic pilot, or they could be capable of basic maneuvers if they were radio controlled from the ground. Killy found no indications either way in his small space.

A dot appeared outside the glass panel. As Killy watched, the dot grew to the size of a bee. From then on, there was no mistaking it. A Cobra killer helicopter slid in along the drone's left wing.

The Cobra stood at 200 yards from the drone. Killy estimated the air speed at 170, but Cobra and drone seemed to hang so still they might have been part of a photograph of the cloudless sky. Only the glint of sun around the Cobra's dull snout gave warning that it was alive and dangerous.

A Cobra has as much to do with the usual helicopter as a cobra has with a garden snake. Low, streamlined, capable of 200 mph, the killer carried four kinds of venom in its rockets, minigun, grenade launcher, and missiles. It could eat the drone in one bite.

Killy guessed what he could about the pilot. It

would have to be one of the foreign officers taking the special course in the Cobras. He would be right-handed, favoring an attack from right the way most novices did. He'd probably shoot wide, too, but with a minigun throwing 4,000 rounds a minute, a pilot didn't have to be a marksman.

A ring of sparklers burst around the Cobra's gun bubble. The red lines of tracers laced the blue sky. The drone banked away from the shells.

It was controlled from the ground, but the drone turned with agonizing slowness. A shell pierced the fuselage over Killy's head, and the drone lurched and steadied itself. The cobra passed to the right side and began sliding back for another run.

Inside the drone, Killy used the dim light from the glass panel and the new hole. A firewall separated him from the control stick, and the wall was sealed. He could hear the Cobra making its second run. Trapped, unable even to get to his knees, Killy rolled with every turn the drone made. When the drone was hit, he lay still and waited for a wing to fall off or the engine to cut out.

A radio box was built into the firewall. The box was solid, probably the only thing salvageable after the drone crashed. He tried to tear the back of the box off and only bloodied his hands. Killy twisted onto his back. On its last pass, the Cobra had ripped open the metal along the top of the fuselage. A strut hung down. He grabbed it and began pulling. The drone swayed from left to right. Killy held onto the strut, his shoulders and legs straining. With a snap, the strut came free.

Killy felt the air around the drone hiss as two rockets bracketed the Cobra's target. He dug one end of the strut into the radio box and pushed the other end. The back of the box flew off, revealing a silver maze of soldered transistors. There wasn't time to read electrical charts that indicated which transistor relayed fuel and altitude information to the ground and which received instructions for speed and turns. Killy used the strut like a spear, slashing the soldered labyrinth apart and ending all contact with the ground. He and the drone were on their own now.

The back of the drone was on fire. Killy paid no attention. The fire would go out when all the paint peeled off. He found the wires running to the ailerons of the wings and tail. Through the gaping wounds on the side of the fuselage, he saw the Cobra sliding forward for the coup de grace.

"Try this," Killy said bitterly.

Spread-eagled, he pulled the upper wire to the left wing and the lower wire to the right wing. Sharply, the drone banked to the right, completely out of the Cobra's path, and two rockets sailed through the open air.

Killy had flown CIA DC-2s and French Mirages, Piper Cubs and B-52s. The drone would have been easy if he didn't have to do it blind and by hand. With its weight-to-power ratio, the drone was highly maneuverable, an unseeing fly with Killy for a brain.

He reversed wires and banked to the left, cutting across the Cobra's path. The helicopter locked on the drone's tail. Killy circled, looping in an Immelman that nearly pulled him off the wires and broke them free. The Cobra filled the air ahead with a thousand shells. Killy climbed over them, hauling on the ailerons. Two more rockets went by in frustration. At the top of his climb, he slipped and the plane stalled, flaming out. Dragging himself up the crawlspace, Killy grabbed the wires again and put the drone in a dive, gathering speed until the rush of oxygen relit the engine's flame. He pulled up level, biting his lip as he heard the drone's echo on the ground below. When he looked through a wound in the fuselage, he saw rows of corn a hundred feet down. Cautiously, he climbed.

He'd beat the minigun and the rockets. The Cobra would use its real weapon now, he knew. The TOW missile could swat down the blind fly with one shot. Score a moral victory for the drone, he thought. Score an Inquisitor for the Cobra.

Of course, he could always jump out of the drone at the last moment, he added to himself with black amusement.

Or ram the Cobra. Who said targets couldn't fight back?

The Cobra was at 3,000 feet because it had expected the drone to crash after its stall. Killy rose toward the helicopter. He soon lost sight of it, but he knew the pilot's pattern by now: swing to the rear and attack from the right. The drone swung into the imagined flight path.

Killy knew he was right when rockets went by the wings as straight and parallel as road stripes. Next, the cannon opened up, shrilly, feverishly throwing a barrier of heavy-caliber shells against the charging drone. The shells smashed open its insensitive nose and drummed on the firewall.

Now, Killy thought, have you got the nerve to fire that missile when your target's right on top of you?

The shells ceased. In their place was the same ugly

buzz he'd heard on the tank field. The missile was in the air and, with their combined speeds, closing near the speed of sound. Killy clung to the wires. The buzz rose to a scream and, suddenly, descended to a low pitch as sound waves stretched in the distance. What made the missile so effective was that it was directed by eye. The Cobra fired, but it didn't have the nerve to sit and guide it home.

Killy let out a long breath. The pilot would be on the radio to the ground by now, demanding who was trying to kill him. Killy could picture his face when the pilot heard the drone was doing it all by itself.

"Like bloody hell," the pilot would say if he were English, "*merde*" if he were French.

Killy let the Cobra slide alongside and wiggled the drone's wings, letting the pilot figure out how a drone could send a distress signal. The Cobra came closer and fired its cannon away from the drone in a tattoo of long and short bursts that spelled out *SOS*. Killy answered with another wave of the wings.

While the pilot yelled into his radio, Killy started diving to the ground. The drone couldn't have more than thirty minutes' fuel and he knew he'd been up in it for twenty minutes, at least. He could sit around while the helicopter exchanged greetings with the ground and the drone's fuel ran out and he dropped like a rock, or he could take it down himself while he still had some control. The main thing to remember was that he had no landing gear. Drones weren't supposed to land.

The Cobra's big favor was that it had shot away enough of the drone's fuselage and firewall for Killy to see ahead. He was still moving at over 150 mph;

there was nothing he could do about that. A patchwork of green pastures and yellow corn fields lay below. He eased down.

The drone coughed as its engine stopped and restarted. The patchwork grew larger, horses and threshers becoming distinct. A highway slid underneath, the windows on the cars glittering like quicksilver. Killy hurdled a high-tension pylon by a hundred feet. The drone's engine hummed sweetly.

Rows of okra showed a shadow of the drone becoming smaller and more distinct. Then Killy was over pasture. The sheep milled, too stupid to be scared. He was fifty feet up. A long field of tall wheat approached. Killy settled down with fifteen feet of clearance and waited.

The wheat field passed, then fields of hay and peas. The engine developed a new cough. Just until the next wheat field, Killy asked it. A gold horizon of wheat grew. Another five seconds, Killy pleaded.

The engine died. The drone dropped like a rock, but a skimming rock. Killy made the wheat field on one bounce.

Rome

FOURTEEN

KILLY AND CELLA walked along the edge of the roof covering the Bernini Colonnade. Forty feet below them on one side were the Piazza of St. Peter and the steps leading up to the church doors. On the nearer side were the papal apartments and the private piazza of the Holy Father called the Belvedere Court.

Cella checked his watch. "It should be any minute now," he commented.

Killy's face was bruised and bandaged. Both men were in cassocks, making them the only dark figures on the roof. The inner edge of the colonnade was lined with stone saints. In the Belvedere Court, two Swiss guards in colorful medieval costume stood with legs spread at the doors of the apartments.

"I could have just stayed in the States, that would have solved the problem," Killy remarked conversationally.

"No. I just would have had to send another Inquisitor after you. Besides, we would have missed you in Rome."

"Really?"

"Of course. Didn't you know you are my favorite? You must have noticed that Romans eat the sweetest pastry but then wash it down with bitter espresso. You are the espresso in my life, my irreverent Inquisitor. Or, perhaps, you were."

The priest checked his watch again.

"We'll see," he added.

From the folds of his cassock he took a long-barreled Italian automatic pistol. Between the thumb and forefinger of his other hand he held one .38-caliber bullet. Expertly, he slid the breech open and placed the shell inside, then slapped it shut. He handed the gun to Killy.

An autumn breeze played around the dome and cupolas of St. Peter's and along the top of the colonnade. Tourist buses moved in low gear around the piazza. Water splashed in the fountains. Killy could almost hear the gears of Cella's watch. Footsteps began walking across the Belvedere Court.

Cella took two steps back. Killy watched the Swiss Guards snap to attention, the round blades of their halberds parallel to their faces. First in view crossing the court was the papal secretary, then two aides. They were talking in muted but animated voices. What they said was lost over the distance to Killy. His eyes shifted behind them.

A slightly bowed figure in white emerged into the court's sunlight. The satin of his cassock dazzled, and on his hand was a ring engraved with the keys of St. Peter. Talking to the Holy Father was a rotund labor leader. The Pope's laugh was high and reedy. It took thirty seconds to cross the court and then the party had passed between the Swiss Guards and gone inside.

One man followed them from the other side of the court, stopping at midpoint and looking up at Cella and Killy. When Cella waved, the man returned the way he had come.

Killy held the automatic out to Cella. The priest watched Killy's unshaking hand for a second before taking the gun.

"I guess I passed," Killy said. "But you had faith in me, that's the important thing."

The two men looked at each other evenly and then Cella shrugged and drew out the hand he had been keeping in his cassock. In it was a Beretta.

"Think of it this way," Cella offered. "We both passed."

Moscow

FIFTEEN

It was November in Moscow. Killy kicked snow from his boots—Russian boots, a bad fit—and waited for the assistant director of the Landau Center for Neurosurgery. A month has passed since his crash on a Kansas farm, time for his ribs to heal and Cella to transform him into a Polish doctor.

"Director Gandurin is coming. Can I take your coat and hang it up?" the receptionist said. She was built like a snow man: sexless, round and cold.

"It's English. I'll hold onto it, thanks."

"You Poles! You think your overcoat would be stolen here?"

"Of course not, Comrade.'"

Reluctantly, she let go of his sleeve. Killy grinned as she clomped back to her desk in front of the door. Luckily, or rather as an example of Cella's planning, the Polish identity fit Killy. To Russians, Poles were outlandish extroverts. She glared at the puddles of melted water forming around his feet.

Director Gandurin was half the size of his receptionist. Black Brezhnev eyebrows danced on his forehead as he welcomed his visitor.

"You were looking for a doctor here?" he asked.

"Yes, a Dr. Cheroff. I am Dr. Kosko and my research is similar to what your assistant was doing?"

"Cheroff?" The eyebrows almost reached Gandurin's hairline. "We have no doctor of that name here. I can show you the staff roster."

"Doctor, I'm a scientist, not a policeman. I came here because in my research I came across a paper in psychosurgery in one of our medical publications. The article was translated from one done, according to the publication, by a Dr. Alex Cheroff of the Landau Center."

"Cheroff? It doesn't sound familiar."

"He was identified as your assistant."

Gandurin suddenly became angry.

"Never. If he was my assistant, I would remember. There was a mistake. Natasha!"

The snow woman behind the desk was Natasha. She rose out of her chair like an avalanche told to attack. Even disguised as a Pole, Killy didn't feel like wrestling with a woman.

"This is not in the spirit of Socialist science," Killy observed as he backed out with his hands up.

"Get out, you and your overcoat," Natasha growled.

Killy complied. Outside, he trudged through the snow, taking his time so that word could pass through the center that someone was interested in the unpopular Dr. Cheroff.

Killy's interest had started on the floor of the Ceros' foyer. He was lying on it and the assistant with the club stood over him, looking at Marie. In Russian, the assistant had blurted out, "What do we do now, Madam Cheroff?"

Killy knew what they did next. They drove to the hangar outside Leavenworth. The million-dollar Cobras were well guarded, but no one kept an eye on the drone targets. After all, they would be destroyed the following day. It was a typical Cero-Cheroff tactic, letting someone else take care of the evidence. The Inquisitor, shaken but not destroyed, had learned a little more about the Cheroffs since then.

Alex Cheroff had been First Assistant at the Landau Center until three years previous when he disappeared. It was assumed he was dead and disgraced. All references to him were deleted from Soviet medical records and publications. He was a non-person, a zero, or "cero" as Cheroff liked to put it.

Maria Cheroff was a dancer in the Moscow Ballet. Her beauty was what kept her in the company; her talent was never in the prima-ballerina class. She also dubbed foreign films into Russian. Both she and her husband were expert linguists. Along with her husband she was presumed to be dead, not living in Kansas. Nobody is ever presumed to be living in Kansas.

Killy turned down Kalinin Prospekt. New skyscrapers lined the wide boulevard and jutted into the gray sky boldly. On the sidewalks, "babushkas," Russian grandmothers, shoveled the snow. Kalinin Prospekt was supposed to be Moscow's answer to Park Avenue. Somebody forgot to tell the babushkas.

He stopped at a tobacco shop for a pack of American cigarettes. He didn't plan to smoke, but he would have seemed odd not to buy them when he could. He also admired the shop's window full of West German pipes.

In the reflection, he saw a man behind him stop to study a streetlight. Much clumsier than the KGB, Killy thought. It would have to be someone from the Center.

At the Melodiya record shop, Killy bought a paper-thin disk of Engelbert Humperdink. Holding his purchase like a gold plate, he went into the Enchantress barbershop. The barbers were women and looked remarkably like barbers around the world. For the equivalent of $4, he got a shampoo, a hot towel on his face, a shave, a razor haircut and enough eau de cologne to halt a moose.

"Just like New York," Killy said, looking in a mirror at the glossy airtight cap she'd made of his hair.

"You've been in New York?" his barber asked with the first words she'd spoken to him.

"Occasionally, I must travel to the United Nations," he said with the right self-importance.

"Have you ever seen John Lindsay?"

Killy sighed, gave her no tip and left with his record. His overcoat had been stolen.

His new friend from the Center was still standing in the snow, supposedly immersed in a *Pravda* account of newer, greater party congresses. Killy went into one of Kalinin's clothing stores.

"Do you want a flashy Swedish overcoat or a good, solid Russian coat?" the salesman asked. He was an old, white-haired man with a pre-Revolution gold tooth.

"How much are they?"

"The good Russian coat is a half, maybe a third what the Swedish rag would cost. They don't have Russian winters in Sweden."

"I'll take the Swedish coat."

The salesman looked at Killy's choice as if he would tear it apart.

"A typical dilettante's decision. All you young people going up and down the Prospekt with your cars and records, forgetting all the sacrifices an older generation has made for you to build the state." The store was full, but all the other shoppers seemed to have heard the speech before. "Can you give me one reason why you chose a foreign coat?"

"The Swedish coat has a lining."

The old man thrust the coat over the counter with disgust for such arguments. Killy put it on and counted out his rubles. The salesman shook his head.

"We only take American dollars," he said.

Wearing his new coat, Killy walked down the Prospekt for the center of town. His shadow from the Center tramped behind, trying to blow his nose on his newspaper.

Killy spoke wearily, each word a puff of condensed air.

"Moscow, Moscow, will you ever change?"

It was snowing again.

SIXTEEN

In the mornings, Killy would come down to the hotel desk, collect his mail and carry it with him to a café for a breakfast of smoked fish and black coffee. The mail had been opened, as he expected and wanted. The letters were from his Polish wife and girlfriend, each asking him to come home in ardent terms and each adding to his cover as a playboy scientist. He was only surprised at the amount of pornographic detail Cella put in the letters.

After breakfast, he went to another of Moscow's scientific libraries in his search for the non-person, Alex Cheroff. Hard-working as they were, the Komitet Gosudarstvennoy Bezopasnosti (KGB) couldn't erase one of the great feats of Russian science: the resurrection of Lev Landau.

Lev Davidovich Landau was the Soviet's leading theoretical scientist, the man who developed mathematical theories explaining the behavior of superfluid helium at temperatures near absolute zero. Much of Russia's space and military programs was a product of the Landau brain. Then a car accident destroyed that brain. Landau received injuries that should have killed him instantaneously. He was pronounced clinically dead half a dozen times, but still Landau and especially the Soviet leaders refused to give up. The best surgeons and neurosurgeons were brought from every part of the Socialist bloc to reconstruct Lev Landau rib by rib and brain cell by brain cell. Cheroff was one of the neurosurgeons summoned.

To a remarkable degree, they succeeded. Lev Landau did live a few years more; the medical journals Killy read in the libraries were proud to point that out. But the remarkable brain, the fragile masterpiece, was irrevocably shattered. Gandurin and Cheroff never were able to release the theories locked forever in the Landau skull, particularly the memory mechanism of the hippocampus. The hippocampus was in the limbic system.

They failed but what they found in their efforts persuaded the Soviet government to fund the Landau Center. Now the Center never heard of Cheroff. Gandurin was more scared than evasive. The Inquisitor was tempted to believe the Russians really didn't know where their non-person was.

After lunch, Killy took long walks through the city. His amateur shadow of the first day was gone, replaced by a team of men from either the KGB or the National Police. No doubt inquiries were being made in Poland about a Dr. Kosko, but Socialist bureaucracies were far more inept than Westerners understood, and it would take weeks for even the secret police to get a firm answer.

Killy played the tourist, going to Red Square and standing in line to enter Lenin's Tomb. He stared over the Kremlin's walls into the minareted citadel where people thought Soviet power centered and then took a short walk to Staraya Ploschad, Old Square, where the power really was: in the Central Committee headquarters of the Communist Party. Guards and a black Zil-144 limousine showed that the Party Secretary, Leonid Ilyich Brezhnev, was in his office.

Footsore, Killy took a cab back to his hotel. His room had been searched, the missing talcum powder on the lip of his bureau drawer told him that much, but Killy didn't care. He poured himself a glassful of vodka, drank it off in one swallow and threw himself into bed.

The next day was bitterly cold. He was sick of libraries and physically bored. From his window, he watched a new, light snowfall covering the city. A taxi stand was across the street. People approached the one taxi at it, haggled over price with the driver and walked away angrily. Moscow taxi drivers were supposed to accept set fares, but Killy had never met one who didn't demand double; the free-enterprise system flourished as long as there were cabs in Russia. Still, Killy was interested. This driver seemed to be out to make a killing.

In his Swedish overcoat, Killy went out into the cold day. He stood on the sidewalk and looked left and right as though he were uncertain where to go. Across the street, the driver read a paperback. Killy went over to the cab.

"Where to?" the driver asked hostilely. Although he was seated behind the wheel, Killy could see the driver was a big man with heavily handsome Tartar features.

"I don't know. I've seen all the sights. Now I'd like to relax and have some fun."

"It's early for girls," the driver answered, while his expression indicated that such things could be arranged.

"No, no. Some sports, diversion."

The driver thought for a moment.

"You want Kropot-Kinskaya Ploschao. They have heated pools there, just like Budapest."

The idea was attractive on a cold Moscow day, but Killy shied away from being trapped indoors. Drowning in a heated pool was no more comfortable than any place else.

"I'd rather something outdoors."

"You like skating?"

Killy nodded.

"Then you want Gorky Park. You should have said so in the first place. From here the price is five rubles."

The price should have been two rubles; Gorky Park was right in the middle of the city. Killy started to walk away.

"Wait, I was just kidding," the driver called. "Four rubles for you."

"Two."

"Three."

Killy got into the back of the cab. After all, it was plain from the way the driver had come down in price that he was waiting for only one customer. As the cab pulled out, Killy looked out the back window. No cars were following, which was wise. It wasn't easy to shadow by car in a city where there were no traffic jams to lurk in.

"You're a Pole. I can tell by your accent," the driver said. "What are you here for? You don't look like a politician."

"Business. But I'm also enjoying myself."

"In Moscow?" the driver looked sharply at Killy through the rear-view mirror. "You Poles have the good life. Open borders, expensive clothes. Have you ever gone to the West?"

"No, but I will someday," Killy said and slapped his hands together. The car's heater was just efficient enough to thaw the front seat. In Rome, the temperature might be all the way down to fifty-five.

They went into Gorky Park where the Moscow River flowed through. Crowds and photographers stood on the banks, shouting and laughing. The cab slowed down.

"See?" The driver pointed into the river. "We call them walruses."

The water was a muddy brown. Some strange forms of life bobbed up and down in it, and Killy realized with a chill that they were swimmers. A river patrol boat cruised slowly by, watching for any of the "walruses" who might, literally, freeze.

"No, thanks," Killy said.

He watched a soldier tumble into the water.

"His friends pushed him," the driver yelled happily.

"Some friends."

"Soldiers do crazy things sometimes."

Killy felt the driver's eyes on him in the mirror. Killy shrugged. The cab pushed through the crowd.

"There are five skating rinks," the driver remarked. "Do you want any in particular?"

"Just take me to the nearest."

Someplace with a crowd, he added silently. The cab finally stopped by a refreshment stand where the driver said skates could be rented. Killy paid the fare.

"That's only three rubles," the driver complained. "I said five."

"Let's call a policeman and let him settle it."

"Bastard."

"Capitalist."

The driver gave Killy the finger and drove off. As the car moved away, Killy had a chance to look around. There was no rink and no crowd, just woods and the falling snow. Nicely done, he complimented the driver. The argument had served its purpose. Killy pushed through the snow to the stand.

A babushka ran the stand. She did rent skates.

"Didn't you know?" she asked. "In the winter we flood the paths through the park. You can skate for miles and miles and not see a soul. So much nicer than the rinks."

Killy looked down the road. Where it curved behind a stand of firs the car had stopped.

"Where would I skate to reach the nearest rink?"

"Just follow the path. The beginners' rink is two miles ahead, and the one for figure skaters is three miles. Are you an expert?"

"No." But he bet the driver was.

Killy found a pair of skates that fit and shoved his shoes into his overcoat pockets. The bulky coat would have been elegant on a rink. It wasn't built for a race through the woods.

"Enjoy yourself!" the old woman called as Killy took his first stride on the ice-covered path.

Russians were not the greatest architects; they brought Italians to build their palaces and Germans to build their factories. But the Russians did have a special feeling for their cold land. The iced trail was skillfully laid out, twisting between copses of snow-laden conifers and then surprisingly emerging into open fields that afforded the skater a vast panorama of the surrounding city. The rooftops of Moscow looked like a fairytale village in a crystal paperweight filled with artificial snowflakes.

Killy concentrated on his skating, his head parallel to his back and his long legs pushing the skate blades into the ice at ninety degrees from his line of movement to get every last bit of speed. Long-unused muscles groaned. As a kid in Boston, Killy had spent whole winters on skates. He didn't get much practice in Rome.

The ice was unscarred, nearly blue against the crisp white of the snow and black trunks of trees. The path curled around a thicket of winter berries and sloped downhill. He looked over his shoulder through the trees at where he had been moments before. The cab driver was on the ice, gaining with expert, powerful strides. In his right hand was a gun.

Killy sprinted onto an undulating meadow, devoid of cover, a part of the park leveled by the German barrage in World War II. The driver followed him down the slope. Skating like a Boston Bruin, Killy drove for the forest 200 yards ahead. He heard a small thunderclap in the near distance and recognized the sound of a medium-caliber gun. A puff of snow shot up ahead of him.

Snow mellowed the German artillery craters, making the meadow unearthly but beautiful, a white sea traversed by two figures skating hard. Killy kept his head low, listening to the rhythmic whoosh of metal on ice and the occasional clap of a firing pin on primer. The two men might have been alone crossing the Arctic, or a nightmare.

A skating figure on uneven terrain was not easy to hit, Killy knew, but he was becoming a bigger target all the time. He could hear the other man's skates. His lead of 100 yards was almost down to 50. With one more hill in the path to cross, Killy squatted down on his skates and turned from one edge of the path to the other as the man behind emptied the automatic's magazine, the sound like a short string of firecrackers.

Past the hill untouched, Killy rose from his squat and built speed for the approaching trees, aware that the cab driver had to reload on the run. The woods were as dark and comforting, its edge as pointed, as a female triangle against a skin of snow. Killy grinned with relief as he darted between the first two trees into the shadows of the forest.

A Central Intelligence agent, or an Englishman from MI-6, or a Frenchman from the Sureté would have stopped behind one of the snow-heavy trees to put a hole in the cab driver, an agent, Killy guessed, of the KGB. It was all a game of counterparts cancelling each other out, linesmen leaving each other for dead for quarterbacks they didn't know and for policies no one understood. Killy had the skill for it but not the heart, or heartlessness. That was why he was an Inquisitor now. He wanted the Cheroffs, not dead men.

The cab driver skated hard, swinging his reloaded gun. The Pole had surprised him simply by staying ahead as long as he did. The woods grew larger, a dark fringe of life encroaching on the dazzling blanket of snow. The first two trees would frame him like a perfect target. The driver cursed and tucked himself into a squat, his gun in his right hand, his left hand on his right wrist.

The winter birds that should have been singing in the woods were silent. The driver watched from side to side warily. The dark trunks and snow clotted boughs and bushes made a shifting screen on each side. The path curved to his left. Abruptly, the Russian slowed and, veering to the edge of the path, grabbed a tree and swung off into the snow. Ahead, where the path curved, he had seen a coat between the trees.

The Russian stepped awkwardly from one tree to another until he had a better view of the man waiting in ambush. There was no mistaking the Swedish coat. The Pole seemed to be kneeling by a bush. The Russian took his time, aiming at the center of the coat, and fired. A neat circle appeared between the coat's shoulders. The Russian fired twice more, adding two more round holes to the coat. The coat shook but didn't collapse. Beginning to understand, the Russian ran through the snow, tripping, in his fury, over his skates so that he crawled the last ten feet.

There was nothing but a coat draped over a bush, the right coat—but minus the Pole. It was a simple trick, but not in the heroic pattern, and the Russian kicked the coat in his disgust.

Far ahead on the ice path, Killy shivered. It wasn't easy to hold on to an overcoat in Moscow.

SEVENTEEN

IN A NEW COAT, Killy blended in with the shoppers around the Yaraslav railroad station. Fruit, stockings, brassieres, beets and stationary were sold in stalls covered by wired-down sheets of corrugated steel. State prices were supposed to be maintained, but the cost of an orange fluctuated by whether police were on the street or not. Killy stepped into a narrow store that sold electroplated picture frames.

"*Shta vih kateeya?*" A salesgirl stepped from the back room through a curtain of colored beads.

"Do you laminate pictures here?" Killy inquired.

"Of course."

He gave her a card he'd picked up on his tour of Red Square. The card had a picture of the exterior of Lenin's mausoleum on one side and a résumé of Lenin's life on the other. The same sort of cards, with a different subject matter, naturally, were sold outside St. Peter's.

"Usually we do pictures of wives or children," she said with a half-smile. "You want this?"

"Please."

The machine was behind the counter. She fed in the card and two strips of plastic. The machine pressed the plastic together and trimmed it. She handed the finished product back to Killy.

"That's thirty kopecks."

He flexed the card between his fingers.

"Do it again, please. I'm not going to be in Moscow every day."

Her expression told him it made no difference to her. The machine gobbled up his card again and spit it out, twice as thick.

"Sixty kopecks."

Killy bent the card and gave it back to her.

"Once more?"

"You must be a Party member. All right."

When he got the card again it was still pliable but hard. Gladly, he paid ninety kopecks.

"I'll carry it close to my heart," he said.

"You had me laminate it three times. I know where you're going to carry it," the salesgirl said cynically.

Killy took a bus to Kalenin Prospekt but avoided the modern avenue to eat supper in a small workers' diner. His meal consisted of cold potatoes in vinegar, a hot stew of potatoes, cabbage with a hint of pork, and a dessert of canned pears that, maybe just by proximity, resembled nothing more than potatoes in syrup. The manager of the diner was Armenian, however, and the coffee was good and Killy drank cup after cup of it as he watched bundled Muscovites go past the diner window toward their apartments and dinner.

It was night when Killy left the diner. In Moscow, night in winter means a hazy polar twilight. He had no trouble finding the Landau Center.

A watchman stood outside the front doors of the Center. There was a stool next to a coal brazier on the top step to the doors, a sign the watchman would not be leaving his post. On one side of the medical center was a building of old apartments, on the other side a vacant lot with a sign declaring that a new addition to the Center would be built on it. Urban renewal was old in Moscow.

Killy chose the apartment house, pressing buttons beside the tenants' names until someone buzzed the front door open. Before anyone could appear and demand to know who he was, the Inquisitor entered and found the cellar stairs. He went through the basement and out its back door to a yard. As he expected, the house fire escape was in the rear. Killy went up the fire escape silently.

At the first window he passed, a whole family of three generations sat around a dinner table, but from baby to babushka they were all looking at the front door, where a man was shouting at his neighbors that hooligans must have pushed the buttons. A cat watched Killy as he passed the second floor while the cat's owner, a tiny lady in a shawl, yelled about hooligans from her apartment door. At the third floor, he passed a young couple in bed who wouldn't have noticed if the Red Army climbed by their window. Killy hoisted himself onto the roof.

The roof of the Landau Center was even with the roof he was on, a ten-foot space separating the two buildings. Killy cleared a path through the snow to the edge of the roof. He'd read Cella's report on him for the Holy Office. Among his so-called special skills was flying planes. Flying without a plane, even a drone, was something else. He took a deep breath and a last look at the Moscow skyline, the bent skyscrapers along Kalenin, the floodlit minarets of Arkhangelsky Cathedral, the massive government offices that might have been found in Washington, and the enormous sea of old, tidy houses where seven million Russians lived.

As a truck went down the street, Killy ran to the edge of the roof and jumped. He made the other roof with inches to spare.

The Center's roof was flat except for an air-conditioner ventilator and an exit built into a shed. Killy took out his laminated card of Lenin's tomb and slipped it into the doorjamb. When the card was halfway in, he twisted it. The door swung open.

Gandurin's office was on the second floor. The director's files were locked, so Killy pushed them away from the wall, unscrewed the back of the metal bureau and released the lock from the inside. Then he pushed the files back to the wall and slid out the drawers from the front. It didn't take long to find what he wanted. Like all bureaucrats, Gandurin kept records for survival's sake.

A good example was a letter dated in the summer of '70:

My Dear Comrade General Rubinoff:

We have received your communication with great distress. Major Kozlov was, as you said, a patient here last year, admitted with a cerebral hemorrhage following an accident. Myself and Dr. Cheroff, my assistant, followed his therapy with personal attention. Every record of that therapy will be made available to any Army commission you designate. Every effort will be made to cooperate. I can assure you, however, that when the major left our center he was examined by Dr. Cheroff and myself and Army physicians and declared to be absolutely recovered. His sudden, irrational actions against the friendly Socialist state of Outer Mongolia comes to us as a surprise and a disappointment. It is unfortunate and I reassure you of our concern. My best fraternal regards,

Anton Gandurin

There were more. A naval commander attempted to send his flotilla against the port of Odessa. A cosmonaut committed suicide, flying his trainer into a research station at Baikonur, the launching complex just fifty miles from Moscow. All the dead men had been treated at the Landau Center. Gandurin's letters became progressively meeker. There were references to investigations into therapy techniques. One of the last letters hinted at what the outcome of those investigations were:

Dear Comrade Superintendent, I would appreciate any mention of our constant and full cooperation with your office. I agree that I, personally, was misled by the viper disguised as my professional colleague, that my lack of judgment endangered not only the security of our armed forces but the future of the entire Socialist world and that such threats to peace cannot be tolerated. At the same time, I would remind you, not for my own sake but for the still important place of psycho-surgery in the modern state, that except for C. [already Cheroff was becoming an unperson, Killy noted] the rest of the Center staff was innocent of wrongdoing and that medical break-

throughs are being made every day by that staff.
All we ask is the opportunity to redeem ourselves
through labor in the field we know best.

Instead of chopping wood in a Siberian labor camp,
Killy added for the director. Somehow the director
had saved his neck and his job, probably because authorities didn't want to fuel the rumors that must have
been stirred by the investigations. More interesting,
the Cheroffs had saved their necks and gone on to bigger and better brain-twisting in the United States. The
possibility that they escaped was unlikely, but the hap-
hazard way they chose their victims at Leavenworth
hardly showed the sort of concerted planning the
KGB was known for.

More and more the suspicion grew in Killy that the
Russians, despite their polar nights, were more in the
dark than he was.

EIGHTEEN

THE ARBAT CAFÉ on Kalinin Prospekt was one of the few sparks of nightlife in town. Killy relaxed at the bar and watched the floor show, a chorus line about as sexy as a group of American high-school cheerleaders.

"Think of it this way," a German on the bar stool next to Killy confided. "Except for the ballet, this is the only place in Russia where you're going to see ten slim girls together at the same time."

It couldn't last forever. The inevitable troupe of balalaika players and acrobats took the chorus girls' place. Most of the audience left and Killy left with them. Not that he had any place in particular to go. His room at the hotel would be watched, and no hotel would admit him at this hour.

Outside, he walked through the streets aimlessly. He left the fashionable Prospekt and meandered through residential neighborhoods, sleepily watching his breath condense in the frosty air. He was almost asleep on his feet when he noticed that he had wandered onto what any city would call Skid Row.

Other countries had addicts; Russia had drunks. Killy saw them huddled in alleys sharing bottles of vodka. He also became aware that one drunk was following him.

"Slow down, brother. Have a drink."

The drunk reeled forward. His two legs disagreed on what order they would step and his arms waved violently, but he lurched through the snow nevertheless, his face dazed and intent at the same time. He carried a bottle of vodka in his hand, and another bottle was stuck in his coat pocket. Two bottles of vodka were a lot for a Russian to afford—the government kept raising the price of a drink—but he was unusually well dressed for an inhabitant of Skid Row.

"I won't have a drink, but I'll help you get home," Killy offered. After all, how many times had his father, the Boston cop, helped Irish drunks to their beds?

The drunk stood still, swaying as he concentrated.

"I don't need help. I'll let you walk me home. But first, let's have a drink."

He held his bottle up and, with great care, unscrewed the top. Then he held the bottle out to Killy. Killy was tempted by the cold to take it but chose not to. Swigging a bottle in the street with a drunk had only so much appeal.

"Come on, I'll walk you home," he said.

"First, a drink."

The drunk stepped forward and threw the bottle at Killy. Killy ducked and the bottle went over his shoulder, smashing against a brick wall. Liquid ran down the bricks, and where it ran the bricks hissed and burned, turning from red to black in seconds. The sharp smell of sulphuric acid cut through the air.

"A drink, you bastard," the drunk said, not so drunk anymore as he pulled out his other bottle of acid.

Killy ran, darting off the sidewalk and between trucks. The man with the bottle followed, taking his time. As Killy looked ahead he saw why; the street was a dead end.

There were cars parked on the street, tiny Zaporozhets and larger Moskviches. Killy tried to break into them, but Russian caution defeated him. To avoid theft, the cars' owners had removed not only windshield wipers and sideview mirrors for the night but also door handles and batteries.

"One last drink, Comrade. Be a sport," the drunk called and roared at Killy's efforts.

Even if Killy did get in a car, all the other man had to do was break the window and throw the bottle in. Killy would be more trapped than ever.

Killy forced open the door of a Zaporozhet through sheer strength. Incredibly, he found the car's ignition key under the seat. He started the compact car up. Before he even put it in gear, the engine died. The owner had drained all the gas. Leering through the window was the drunk, the bottle in one hand and a brick in the other. Killy dove through the side door, scrambling through a drift of snow that was up to his waist. The drunk circled the rear of the car, cutting off escape as if he were herding a sheep.

At the dead end of the street was a blank wall without doors or windows. Empty bottles and trash scarred the snow. Killy ran by a stripped panel truck standing on blocks, then stopped. There was nowhere left to go. He picked up a bottle and, holding it by the neck,

smashed half of it off, leaving him with a jagged weapon. Unconcerned, the other man unscrewed the lid on
his second bottle of acid. When Killy threw the broken
bottle in desperation, the drunk sidestepped it easily.

Killy picked up another bottle. The men were fifteen
feet apart. The drunk watched Killy stuff a handker-
chief in the top of the bottle and shake it. Killy lit the
ready-made wick with matches he'd picked up at the
Arbat.

"You're bluffing." The drunk shook his head. "If there
was any vodka in that bottle, one of the bums on this
street would have found it long ago."

"You picked up a lot of slang in Kansas."

The drunk paused.

"The new face is good," Killy remarked, "but when
you smile you show your teeth. I saw that steel tooth
too many times in the Cero basement not to recognize it. I suppose Cheroff's many talents don't stretch
to dental work. Where are the Cheroffs?"

"You're in no position to ask."

Killy glanced at the flaming wick.

"Where are they?" he repeated.

The other man felt his bottle growing slippery in his
hand. He knew there was a liter of acid in his hand,
he told himself, and there was only a remote possibility that Killy's threat of a Molotov Cocktail was real.
Viscerally, he realized Killy's bottle was no fake. But
years as Cheroff's assistant, of intellectual rigor, answered that he was in no danger. He cocked his arm to
throw the acid.

Killy threw first, underhand as if he were fast-pitch-
ing a softball. The bottle hit its target in the stomach.
The scientist staggered, not drunkenly but stunned.
The air around him quivered and then fire became vis-

ible, a blue shroud over his clothes. He dropped the acid as he tried to tear off his vodka-soaked coat, but flames leaped to his shirt and skin. Screaming, he ran from Killy, clawing as he ran at the flames around his neck, the fire burning and suffocating him simultaneously. His hair, groomed with the usual Russian alcoholic cologne, burst on fire.

Across the open end of the street, the headlights of three cars suddenly lit and blocked the road. Killy ran after the burning man, trying to throw snow on him. A third man ran from the cars.

Cheroff's assistant shuffled on his knees, the rags of his clothes sagging around a blackened torso and head. Killy kicked him forward into the snow and started trying to cover the flames. He had an armful of snow when the third man reached them, shoved a gun to the burning man's head and fired.

Flames licked the charred body. Killy dropped the snow in his hands.

"Poor idiot," the man with the gun said and then transferred his attention to Killy, who recognized him. It was the cab driver.

NINETEEN

At 8 p.m., a train of fourteen coaches pulled out of Yaraslav Station. The curtains of its windows were lace, and on the sides of the sleek cars were plaques announcing in three languages the train's main stops: Moscow, Ulan Bator and Peking. In six days it would travel 4,890 miles, nearly a fifth of the circumference of the earth.

Viktor Gogol slapped Killy on the knee as the station rolled by their compartment window.

"Well, Kosko, or whatever your name is, did you ever think we would be taking a trip together to Peking?"

"We wouldn't be if you weren't such a crummy shot."

"Ah, you're just tough to kill. We know that. You're a professional like me. No hard feelings, I hope. I'm the one who looked like a fool, shooting at an empty coat. The only thing we could never figure out was your agency. You don't care to tell me now that we're alone?"

Gogol had dark eyes and a swarthy, wide face. Killy had the feeling that the Russian agent treated most people with amiable contempt—the Tartars had ruled Russia for hundreds of years—but the unknown quantity of a Killy Gogol treated as an equal.

"Confidentially, I'm an Egyptian agent," Killy whispered.

"If you were Egyptian this train would be going to Tel Aviv." Gogol laughed. "So you won't tell me. Agreed. We will help each other and then you go your way and I go mine. It's an even exchange, no? I know where the Cheroffs are and you know what they look like now. After all, neither the Americans nor us want these maniacs running free."

"I'm no maniac. You tried to kill me in Corky Park."

"Agh, I explained that. Cheroff was doing his operations in league with some military hardliners and a faction of political fanatics. You Americans always seem to forget that just like you have your FBI and crazy men in the CIA who want a war to destroy the world, we have the same problems. They thought if they could create enough turmoil in our space programs and on our borders, then the Central Committee would be frightened into giving them more power. Stalinists, Trotskyites, the officer corps is full of them. You know, we were left with eighty thousand generals after fighting the Germans. We still have thousands of them senile as mad old dogs."

"Not half as senile as your story."

Gogol wasn't insulted. He leaned back in his chair and regarded Killy with interest.

"All right, my friend. You tell me what happened."

One of the Chinese stewards came into the room with tea. With the exception of the dining car the train was run by Chinese. The stewards wore blue Mao suits, and in the corridors were framed photos of Chinese peasants at work in the field and captions with quotations from the Chairman. The two giant Communist states no longer had diplomatic relations, but nothing yet had interfered with the Moscow-Peking Express.

"You people," Killy said when the steward was gone. "You in the KGB."

Gogol kept an impassive face, but his pupils dilated.

"Go on."

"It's an old trick of the secret police. One faction of the agents work for the hardliners. One faction spies for the middle-of-the-road politicians like Brezhnev. The third faction works for the liberals. That way, no matter who wins out in the Central Committee, the KGB always comes out on top."

Gogol looked out the window at the suburbs of Moscow.

"You make some sense," he conceded. "We like to keep in touch with different elements."

"The hell with that. The KGB likes to keep in control. You're your own little government. You infiltrate the Party cells, rule the Russian Orthodox Church, let one liberal publish in the West and kill another. The Cheroff operation smells of the KGB. Treason in the officers corps wouldn't give more power to the Army, only to the secret police. And the Army couldn't have smuggled him out of the country. Only you people could."

Gogol sipped his tea. "Personally," he said, "I prefer Peter and the Wolf as a fairytale." His eyes looked shrewdly over the lip of his cup. "But, saying that your theory has some relation to reality, you would know

that any of our agents implicated with Cheroff have
been purged. There is no reason for the Americans to
hold us responsible for what happened at their war
college. That would be most uncomfortable for everyone. It was just to quiet rumors about what occurred
at the Landau Center that we wanted to eliminate you.
Just so you understand."

"Oh, I understand perfectly."

Bound by such expressions of mutual trust, the two
agents rode on to China, where the KGB had again
found the trail of Alex and Maria Cheroff.

By dawn of the next day, the train was past the Ural
Mountains and 500 miles from Moscow. A sense of
routine was already settling in. The Russian-run dining
car offered unwashed tables and a long menu of un-
available meals. Except for meatballs; meatballs appeared under the names of ham and eggs, steak, or
fish. Soon, everyone avoided the diner, satisfying themselves with Chinese tea until the train stopped at a
way station, where they could buy sausages and fruit
from cunning babushkas. During the stops, the Chinese stewards washed the outside of the cars. If the ever-
present Soviet soldiers were embarrassed by the con-
trasting griminess of the dining car, they didn't show
it. While they worked, the stewards sang, "The East
Is Red."

Killy was surprised to discover that there were few
Russians or Chinese among the passengers. There were
some East Europeans and American students, but
most of the travelers were Mongols and Vietnamese.
Except for the students, who gushed over everything,
everyone regarded everyone else with polite aloof-
ness. Killy and Gogol passed the time playing backgammon.

By the third day, the train was 1,000 miles from Moscow, rolling through endless birch-tree forests. Sverdlovsk, a giant step of Soviet planning, a city of gleaming apartment houses topped by television aerials, was stamped in the middle of the forest.

"I saw Seattle once from a trawler," Gogol said. "Just the same."

Two passengers were picked up in Sverdlovsk, giggling Mongol exchange students, both girls. They were put in the compartment next to the agents'. The train had just pulled out again when they visited.

"Come in." Gogol waved expansively. "We two were getting tired of looking at each other's face. Besides, I hate losing money at backgammon."

The girls were alike as twins, pretty, with round faces and their hair in pony tails. The slightly taller one was Ude, the slightly shorter one was called Shanda. Neither Gogol nor Killy could pronounce their last names. The girls' Russian was good, though—a result, they explained, of the language being mandatory in Mongol schools.

"Now we are graduated and have to go home," Ude pouted. "We will miss our boyfriends."

"Sad," Gogol commiserated.

"They're kids," Killy warned the Russian in Polish.

"They graduated. They're ready to take their place in glorious Socialist womanhood," Gogol answered in the same language, and then asked the girls in Russian if they understood Polish.

Ude and Shanda giggled.

The four of them stayed in the compartment, growing ever more friendly and sharing a supper of peaches and plum wine. Together, they watched night fall on the cities of Omsk and Novosibirsk, and then the train was lost again, like a time machine, in the eternal Russian forests.

"I forgot to put my luggage up on the rack," Ude told Killy. "Could you help me?"

Reluctantly, because he knew what was coming, Killy agreed. They went into her compartment. The suitcases were already up on the rack.

Ude closed the door. "You're much better looking than my boyfriend."

"Ude, I don't want to embarrass you . . ."

"I know what I'm doing."

She unbuttoned her student's tunic. Her body was slim, a soft yellow, the breasts small with brown tips. She put her hand boldly between Killy's legs.

"And I know what you're thinking. I can feel it," she said. "You're bigger than my boyfriend, too."

"He'd be pleased to know you're thinking of him."

"He knows how I love sex." She pulled down the zipper of Killy's pants and slid her hand inside. He stepped back. "What's the matter? You don't like girls? Are you prejudiced against Mongols."

"Nothing like that. I like you. Honestly, you're a little young for me."

Anger tightened her almond eyes.

"Young people are the leaders of the Revolution! We make the policy of the people. We seize power because power is rightfully ours. All who disagree are bourgeois reactionaries and enemies of the people."

Killy considered his position.

"Well, if you say so," he concluded and helped Ude out of her pants.

Through the night, the express added more miles from Moscow, penetrating deeper and deeper into the dark Asian heartland of Russia. Killy felt the tempo of the wheels through Ude's body, her spread thighs and flat stomach rocking back and forth, her hard, brown nipples vibrating. As the train braked around a mountain, she hissed with pleasure. Their compartment window fogged with the heat of their bodies.

As dawn hit the window, Killy reached over Ude and wiped the glass. They looked down at Lake Baikal, the largest fresh-water lake in the world. Absentmindedly, he patted Ude's buttocks.

"We're almost to Mongolia. You must be happy."

"Not because I'm almost home, Doctor." She pressed herself against him.

"I wish you wouldn't do that. Call me doctor, I mean."

"Do you mind if I do this?"

"Next you'll ask me if I'm ticklish there."

Killy slapped her rump and got off the bunk. Ude pursed her lips in disappointment, then jumped off the sheets and ran around the train compartment searching for her clothes. There was nothing immature about her body, but when she had her student's tunic back on, Ude looked again like a kid.

They had breakfast with Gogol and Shanda. The Russian showed the same sexual satiation Killy felt. The girls giggled together more than ever. Lake Baikal continued to slide past their window.

"Why are you going to China?" Ude asked in between bites of cheese and bread.

"Trade agreements," Gogol answered.

"What kind?"

"We're trading my Russian friend for his weight in rice," Killy yawned. He hadn't had much sleep during the night.

The girls were not pleased.

"Don't treat us as children," Shanda warned him. "Answer our question."

"He's like that." Ude frowned. "Never serious."

"A Pole," Gogol explained.

"Call me when we reach Warsaw," Killy said as he closed his eyes and lay down.

Finally, Lake Baikal came to an end and the train turned south along the Selenga River. The steward brought meals to the compartment, and late at night the train and its odd bedfellows crossed the Russian-Mongolian border, where everyone had to disembark for customs. In a hall decorated by a golden bust of Sukhe Bator, the Mongolian Lenin, every suitcase was examined with excitement for every unusual article. One of the American students had a diaphragm. The more she explained its employment the more excited the Mongolians became. At last, her face red, she surrendered the mysterious diaphragm and ran to the train in tears. The Mongols loved it.

"At least, we got rid of the Russian dining car," Killy said when the train was under way again. "God, I'm starved."

Gogol didn't take offense. Rather, he led the way to the new diner, where they discovered that only Mongolian tughriks were accepted in payment.

"We weren't allowed to exchange rubles at the border," Gogol protested.

Shanda and Ude went at once back to the compartment. Killy pulled Gogol off the waiter.

"Don't be a fool and start a fight."

Gogol, furious, weighed himself against Killy.

"Look, Pole, I still don't know who you are. But I want you to understand that I am in command. I missed you once, I may not a second time."

"You are a fool," Killy said and left the diner.

Ude was in her compartment drinking tea when Killy returned. She was uncharacteristically quiet and he was content to take a cup and gaze out the window at a flat country and a night full of new constellations. Every ten miles or so they would see the light of one of the squat tents called yurts that most Mongols lived in.

"We reach Ulan Bator in the morning and you get off then, don't you?" Killy said.

In the corridor Gogol stamped by to the other compartment.

"Drink your tea. You must be hungry," Ude said. In the next compartment, Killy heard Shanda trying to placate Gogol with the same offer.

"Damn," Killy cursed as a bump on the tracks made him spill the hot tea on his pants. "Look at that. Could you get a towel from the washroom for me?"

Ude rushed out. As soon as the door was closed, Killy stood on his chair and pulled down her suitcase, opening and throwing its contents on the floor. What he was looking for was on top of the pile: a page written in Mandarin Chinese for the identification and murder of Gogol and himself.

He let it lay where he found it and waited by the door. Ude came in. She wasn't carrying a towel because she didn't think she was going to use it. Her eyes traveled from her suitcase to Killy and her mouth opened to scream.

Killy's hand shot out and closed over her face. His other hand swung her onto a chair. As she struggled to get free, he picked up the tea pot and shoved its spout into her mouth, pouring its contents down her throat.

Ude fought for another thirty seconds, then her hands lost their coordination, her eyes became glassy, and she hung limply in his grasp.

The girl's pockets were empty. Killy searched the chair she had been sitting in when she offered him tea. From between the chair curtains he took a syringe and a small bottle of clear liquid. The label didn't describe any poison but something better: synthetic agglutinogen. Agglutinogen was the clotting factor in blood. It would save the life of a hemophiliac. One injection of it into normal blood would create a clot that, once it reached the brain, meant a natural, instantaneous death.

Killy dove into the corridor and into the next compartment. Shanda was over Gogol's inert body, preparing to push her hypodermic needle into the Russian's arm. Killy pulled her off by her hair. She swung the needle at him. He caught her wrist and squeezed until her fingers opened and the needle dropped. His other hand closed on her throat, holding her with her feet swinging in the air until her eyes rolled back. Shanda folded up on the floor. Killy peeled a sock from her foot and stuffed it in her mouth.

"Up, you clown," he grunted as he heaved Gogol to the window. A freezing wind filled the compartment as he pushed the window down. Gogol sagged, his head lolling from side to side.

Killy drove his fist into the Russian's stomach and shoved Gogol's head out the window. Gogol heaved and caramel-colored vomit poured into the night and over the side of the railroad car. Killy supported him until Gogol's stomach was empty and then dropped him over a chair.

The Inquisitor leaned on the open window, letting

the fresh air hit himself. There was more to clean up than a little vomit. When Gogol came around he would insist on killing the girls. Not that Gogol ever saw the signs that they were something more than nymphomaniacs. Killy had suspected Ude since he noticed that one of the many Chinese pictures in the railroad corridors carried Red Guard quotations that were the same as her angry undressing speech. If Gogol hadn't been in the same compartment, the Russian still should have wondered why Ude and Shanda wanted to spend the trip in bed, why they wanted to know so much about Killy and Gogol and, most obvious, why two Mongolian girls who had made the trip before wouldn't bring their own national currency to eat in a Mongol dining car. Of course, he reminded himself ruefully, Gogol didn't have Maria Cheroff to prepare him for Ude and Shanda.

Killy rubbed his face wearily. It would be sunrise in two more hours and they would be in Ulan Bator, the Mongolian capital. Gogol would dispose of the girls before then, strangle them and throw their bodies out of the train.

Killy drummed his fingers on the window, then he shoved it all the way open. Ahead, he could see the last mountain range they would pass through before the last, long descent to Ulan Bator. The train was already beginning to slow.

Five minutes later, when the Moscow-Peking Express was climbing the mountain grade, Shanda went out the window. A moment later, Killy threw Ude out from the other compartment. Their suitcases and clothes followed, flying through the air into a countryside with more wild camels than people. With luck, the girls could ride to town in a couple of days.

A hard night's work done, Killy threw himself on his bed for a few hours' sleep. His last thought was wondering what the Mongols at the border were doing with a diaphragm.

Tsining

TWENTY

In winter, the predominate impression of Moscow is an institutional gray softened by the ever-present snow. The color of Peking is brown, the brown of bare brick housing and the brown of dust from the Gobi desert which continually falls on the city in such quantities that a quarter of the inhabitants wear surgical masks.

Besides masks, the people wear blue tunics and quilted, loose-fitting pants. The drivers of horse-drawn drays wear them, students on pedicarts wear them, lovers wear them and the Chinese security agent following Gogol and Killy away from the Nationalities Hotel down Changan Boulevard wore them.

"They probably heard from those Mongolian girls," Gogol swore. "Why didn't you kill them? What kind of an agent are you?"

"If the Chinese government knew as much as those girls did, they never would have let us off the train. They put security men on the American students, why shouldn't they on us? You're just disgruntled because you lost your contact."

All foreign visitors to Peking registered at the Nationalities Hotel, which made it the KGB's most convenient message "drop." A clerk in the Russian hire spotted the arrival of the Cheroffs from the United States, not by their faces but by the amount of tell-tale scientific material they brought with them. Shortly afterward, the Cheroffs and the clerk all disappeared.

In Tienanmen Square, the two agents saw the European and American passengers from the train, who were queuing for a guided tour of the Great Hall of the People and the Revolution and History Museums. Killy and Gogol and their shadow in the surgical mask passed by.

"Let's take a bus," the Russian suggested.

"We can walk faster than a bus in this city. This is the only city in the world where traffic police are on the side of the glorious masses of pedestrians."

The center of Peking was made alive by the banners along Tienanmen Square and parks invitingly named Central Lake, Joyous Pavilion and Temple of Heaven. Killy and Gogol were soon in a zone of Russian-gray government buildings, though, and halted at a nondescript door with no title.

Inside, they were expected and led through a hall past a hundred cubicle-sized offices to one no different from the rest. In that office they were told to wait. They did as they were told for one hour and then two.

"Bastards." Gogol crushed his empty cigarette pack. "Now they're all going to go to lunch and leave us here. If we go eat, they'll say we insulted them."

At three o'clock, after they had waited five hours,

Killy and Gogol were joined by a middle-aged administrator and an interpreter. The Chinese treated them with a disdain verging on imperial, letting their visitors stand or sit where they wished.

"There is important work being done here at the Bureau of Mines. Mr. Chi says that he has little time for you."

Killy recognized the speaking interpreter as the man who had followed them behind a mask and knew that Gogol did too. No doubt, the interpreter was even aware of their recognition, but he didn't show it any more than they did. That was how business was transacted between the Communist giants.

"I am Dr. Gogol of the Soviet Bureau of Mines . . ."

"There are no doctors or other titles in a true people's democracy," the interpreter interrupted.

". . . and this is my associate, Comrade Kosko of the Polish People's Republic," Gogol went on unruffled. "He has come to discuss possible improvements in technology."

Chi unbent a little. "The Chinese People's Republic recognizes the PPR as a friendly people without imperialist aspirations. However," he said through the interpreter, "we want the Polish government to realize that the Pamir Mountains ruby mines and the surrounding territory are the rightful and historic property of the Chinese people."

Killy had expected the qualified welcome. The Pamir Mountains were on the westernmost Soviet-Sino border directly above Afghanistan, and in those mountains the Russians and Chinese kept an uneasy truce so that each could get a share of the high-quality rubies mined there.

"We have reason to believe that there are violations

of our agreement concerning the stones," Gogol said.

"The Chinese people are peace-loving. There have been no violations."

"Peace-keeping Soviet troops have found the demarcation lines moved."

"The Chinese people claim only what is theirs."

"The Russian people will not cede one foot of their fatherland. They will make mining the stones impossible if violations continue," Gogol persisted. "As you are aware, the Russian people and the great Indian people have forged new friendships. The Indian people are willing to supply whatever gems we are unable to mine in the Pamir works."

"The Indian running dogs are expansionist adventurers. Our new friends in Pakistan will supply whatever we lose from Pamir."

"In low-quality stones," Gogol remarked.

The point was well taken. Sapphires and rubies were simply different colored variations of the same pure stone called corundum, the hardest mineral next to diamonds. Even low-quality corundum was a perfect abrasive for commercial use, but high-quality stones were necessary for use as jewelry or, far more important, in many areas of scientific research.

Chi tapped a pencil on his desk. The security agent who was the interpreter took the lead.

"It is the policy of the People's Republic that there be no compromise with the Soviet revisionists. At the same time, however, the Chinese people keep promises made. If, in fact, there have been any violations, they will be investigated."

"I want that in writing." Gogol jabbed his finger at the Chinese.

"Such a written statement might be miscontrued as

an admission that such violations had taken place," Chi protested without waiting for the charade of a translation. "I will not consider it."

"Not only do I demand it, but I also demand an accounting of the stones taken from your mines as stipulated in the mutual audit agreement governing the mines."

The Chinese's expression turned from concern to bemusement.

"My friend, neither side has submitted an accounting for five years," Chi explained. "Why should we do so now for you?"

Gogol opened the briefcase he'd brought.

"I brought all our figures from Moscow for your inspection. Now I demand to see yours in return. Don't forget, however, that this is only a procedural difficulty. The real purpose of my trip is to secure your statement on border violations."

Chi and the security man looked at each other, then Chi stood.

"You will have your answer. I must consult with other authorities."

Chi left and returned an hour later with the interpreter. In the latter's hands were heavy accounting books. Chi was smiling.

"We are ever eager to cooperate. You may submit your accounts and examine ours in this office, on the condition that you rescind your request for the statement concerning alleged violations. Otherwise, I cannot help you."

Gogol took a long time to consider.

"If you give me your oral agreement that such violations will cease."

"Oral? Of course." Chi beamed. "Consider that you have it."

Gogol and Killy had what they wanted. The Chinese thought their visitors would be able to read off only the numbers of gems, but within an hour Killy had read the trend of high-quality ruby distribution throughout Communist China. Walking back on Changan Boulevard, he told Gogol what he'd found.

"The only important figures were the most recent ones, where the Cheroffs could affect the flow. His lasers need a stockpile of the very best rubies. Within the past weeks, there has been a sharp increase in rubies going to Tsining."

"Tsining? That's in the middle of nowhere." Gogol shook his head. "The Chinese have nothing there but a big army base."

"Gogol, old man, you ought to try Kansas sometime."

TWENTY-ONE

KILLY TRAINED his glasses on the exercise field. He'd come full circle. With one or two differences.

The war trophies lining the main road of the People's Liberation Army Two Hundredth Division's Tsining camp were American artillery pieces and tanks captured in Korea.

There were no Dairy Queens or pizza parlors. Instead, the division's 10,000 men had tilled self-sufficient farmlands in the dry earth.

And instead of Leavenworth's draftees spraying M-16s, Tsining's volunteers trained on the exercise field in medieval, armorlike leather breastplates and iron masks as they thrust at each other with wooden staffs. Not that they didn't have more modern weapons. On the firing field, Killy had already seen the Chinese version of a TOW missile destroy the mockup of an American tank.

"Look." Gogol jabbed Killy's shoulder for attention. "Those personnel carriers we saw before. They're not personnel carriers. They're mobile missile launchers."

Killy looked where the Russian pointed and saw that the rear half of the truck had been raised to expose a forty-foot missile on its sled.

"Irkutsk," Gogol said. "They can't reach Moscow with a modified Sark missile like that. If they hit Irkutsk they cut Siberia from the rest of Russia." He looked at Killy. "They plan a war of attrition against us, you know, because they are five hundred million more people. Without our Siberian fuel, we would lose."

Killy and Gogol were on the fringe of the camp in a bare box on stilts that was the marking tower for a heavy machine-gun firing range.

"If the Cheroffs get hold of the commissar of Irkutsk, we lose," Gogol added.

"Don't flatter yourself. Russia is not in the generals' minds at this camp."

Killy watched a truck draw up outside a low, white building near the center of the camp. Like many Chinese camps, this one had its own pharmaceutical factory. The equipment being unloaded from the truck had nothing to do with drugs, however, and Killy saw a new generator being installed on the exterior of the building. He kicked Gogol with his foot.

"Quick. Look at the white building."

Standing outside, checking the condition of his new equipment, was Alex Cheroff. A Chinese soldier of advanced age was at his side. When the soldier spoke, the men handling the equipment jumped.

"General Li Peng-fei, or Comrade Li, since there are no ranks in the PLA," Killy said. "Those are cathode ray tubes. Well, that finally explains why they let us come here from Peking. They probably think we're dead by now."

"What do you mean?"

"I mean, Peking has no control in this part of China. It's been that way since the Cultural Revolution. Li heads the army faction that thinks Mao is dead. The traveling papers Peking gave us, the ones they thought we were going to use, would have been our death sentences. Melodramatic, isn't it?"

"Just Chinese," Gogol scoffed. "So why would the Bureau of Mines give Li the stones he wanted?"

"Because there are camps all around the country just like Li's. Peking isn't ready for another revolution, so they try to keep the generals content while they build new divisions in the capital. Now, look at the battalion flags on the barracks. See the gold one with the red book in the center? That's the flag of the University of Peking's Red Guards. When the Cultural Revolution came to an end, the university Red Guards wouldn't believe it and made a fort out of the school buildings. The Peking authorities had to use an attack force of factory workers to drive the students out, but the kids fought their way to the countryside, to this camp. This is where Ude and Shanda came from."

"And how do you know that?"

"I only suspected it until we got here. The labels on the bottles of agglutinogen were from the Two Hundredth Division's pharmaceutical factory."

Gogol dropped his glasses and slid down to the platform floor. He rested his head on the weathered wooden guardrail a long time staring at Killy before he spoke.

"You filthy anonymous bastard. You knew all along where Cheroff and his wife were ever since the train. And you made me go through that performance in Peking." He took his automatic from his coat and aimed it at Killy. "Why didn't you tell me before?"

"That's one reason. You would have killed me once you didn't need me. Besides that performance of yours was necessary for the Chinese to let us come here."

"I could kill you now."

"Too much noise."

"There are other ways than a gun."

"Chancy, Gogol, very chancy."

Slowly, the Russian slid the safety catch back on the Walther. Killy went back to watching the army camp. Outside a mess hall, the soldiers gathered for the evening meal. Even at a distance, Killy was able to smell vats of bean curd and vinegar.

"All right," the Russian said resignedly, "since the KGB finds itself following your plans anyway, how do we get the Cheroffs out of there? We have to try it tonight."

They ducked down as a PLA helicopter fluttered by to the camp landing strip.

"You pointed it out yourself, Gogol. By rocket."

Night and temperature fell together. The dark revealed what was important to General Li and the PLA's Two Hundredth Division. Floodlights emerged around the division headquarters, helicopter pads, missile launchers and pharmaceutical factory. Killy and Gogol climbed down from the marking tower and ran in a crouch through the target setters' trenches. The ground underfoot crackled with frost. During the summer, the temperature on the Manchurian plain fell from 110 degrees to 40. In winter it fell from 40 degrees to 10 below zero.

"First alarm wire," the Russian whispered as they crossed from the firing range to an open field. He pointed out a trip wire six inches from the ground.

They stepped over it and traversed a plowed field of peas. At the other end was another trip wire and a road leading to the Sark launcher.

"Mine field," Killy said.

Faint depressions dotted the road. The harder they looked, the more of the round depressions they could see all around them.

"Now what?" Gogol asked.

"It's a mobile launcher. They move it around. Look for tire marks."

The freezing earth cracked, displaying the wounds made by a forty-ton missile and launcher. The two agents followed the tracks, wending their way through the mines to within 500 yards of the Sark. They lay down, watching and listening.

"A machine gun nest at a hundred yards on the left," Gogol said after a half an hour.

"Same on the right. No dogs."

"They eat dogs. Well, Comrade, which way do you want to go in, left or right?"

"In between."

"Left," Gogol answered. Before Killy could stop him, the Russian was up and running in an easy lope to the machine-gun nest on his side.

Killy waited ten minutes and followed. There were three men in the nest when he arrived. Two were Chinese. They were draped over their gun, dead, puncture wounds oozing at the back of their necks. Gogol was alive, cleaning his knife.

"So you'll remember that we are full partners," the Russian said softly. He and Killy put on the dead soldiers' quilted overcoats and fur-lined hats. Side by side, they marched toward the missile launcher.

Through the increasing glare of converging floodlights, Killy and Gogol stepped in the lock-kneed style of the PLA. The Russian's Tarter blood made him look Chinese enough in the blinding lights. Killy trusted Irish luck and the professionalism of the Chinese guards; there was no reason among true believers and little reason to look twice at comrades.

"Liquid-fueled," Gogol whispered with excited surprise.

A technician making a routine check of the missile's fuel valves straightened up. The "democratic" officer in charge, devoid of emblems of rank, stepped forward.

"Why are you leaving your post?"

"Sick," Killy answered.

"You don't look sick."

"You handle the missile and leave the men to me," Gogol said from the side of his mouth. "I know how you hate to kill."

Gogol began shifting the AK-47 he'd taken from the dead guard off his shoulder.

"I don't know you," the officer said. His hand moved to his revolver.

Gogol swung the submachine gun down on the officer's hand and unloaded a burst through the man's stomach. Killy broke for the launcher. The Russian was down on one knee, spraying a field radio and the man trying to operate it, then wheeling to cut down four soldiers who were running to their officer's aid. As they fell, he turned to the floodlights, shattering them one by one and throwing one half of the missile position into darkness.

Killy caught the technician jumping down off the Sark and broke the technician's arms against the launcher's sled. A second technician ran from the fuel tanks with a rifle. Killy rolled under a tire and caught the man from behind, driving his straightened fingers into the Chinese's kidneys. Crippled, the technician still managed to fire his rifle, but Killy had kicked the barrel back and the single bullet that left it carried most of the firer's head up into the night. The launcher's driver leaped out of his cab with a rifle and landed dead from a burst of Gogol's AK.

Ten-foot-tall cylinders of liquid oxygen sweated beside the launcher. Killy followed their metal tubes to the poised missile. Astride it, he twisted the valves full open and then pulled the valves off. Gauge needles began an inexorable climb into the red.

He jumped as reinforcements began firing from the other side of the launcher. Gogol was happily lying down, shooting under the missile and chopping down the nearer rescuers.

"Let's go!" Killy yelled.

They ran in a semicircle around the site. Behind them, the Chinese fired at each other. From the dark a pair of headlights approached.

"An armored car!" Gogol exclaimed. "One of our old models."

Killy ran in front of the vehicle, waving his arms. The car stopped, and as soon as it did Gogol came from the side and emptied the rest of his submachine gun into the driver and gunner. He pulled the bodies out and dumped them in the dark. A cord ran on poles by the car and led the way through the minefield. Killy and Gogol got in, turned the car in a tight circle and drove back to the camp, following the cord with their lights.

"The firing's stopped. How much time do we have?" Gogl asked.

"They'll try to turn the valves back, but they won't be able to. Then they can try breaking the feeding tubes, but that would only ignite the oxygen sooner. They'll start running soon."

The armored car lurched through the dark, always within a foot of the safety of the cord. Behind, a thousand pounds of pressure forced a flood of explosive liquid oxygen into the missile, straining its tanks and growing colder, freezing and warping metal, turning a missile into a bomb.

Gogol stood up in the gunner's turret and checked the 50-caliber machine gun.

"Nothing's happening yet," he called down. "Are you sure you knew what to do?"

In answer, the armored car tilted on its front wheels. A sensation like the city collapsing compressed their eardrums. Over his head, Killy could faintly hear Gogol swearing over and over. Killy looked back out the window.

It was as if the sun had risen early. Flames reached hundreds of feet into the sky, angry black and red balls of it turning like the creation of the universe, propelled up by new explosions as the fuel cylinders joined in, oxygen feeding on air so that one half of the sky seemed to light. Parts of the missile and launcher began landing a thousand feet from the explosion around the armored car.

"Like an atom bomb." Gogol continued to stand in the turret and stare.

The atomic warhead couldn't go off until it was armed, Killy knew. Though that wouldn't comfort the soldiers trapped around what had been a missile and was now a holocaust. He crossed himself and pushed his foot on the accelerator.

Trucks with fire control equipment raced past them in the opposite direction. They were out of the mine-fields, and stunned sentries waved the armored car by checkposts. Sirens cried throughout the camp as Killy entered the gate.

"We need more soldiers at the launcher," he shouted without halting.

General Li rode past in an armored car at the head of trucks of men. Some of the Chinese yelled at Killy for an explanation of what happened, but the sirens muffled their voices. He weaved the car through a con-fusion of traffic to the pharmaceutical laboratory, stop-ping and jumping out to bang his fist on the door.

"Russians, Russians!" he shouted.

The door opened to the width of an eye. In the chaos of sirens and rushing soldiers, the eye held no recogni-tion of Killy.

"Comrade Li says come with us," Killy ordered in Russian broken by Chinese.

"Is it a raid?"

"Come now."

"My papers and equipment."

"Now!"

The door shut. Killy stood by it for what seemed an eternity. Gogol watched from the car turret, casually moving the machine gun at the assembling squads. The camp sirens continued to howl.

"My work. I can't leave my work," Cheroff explained as he came out of the door with a hastily packed crate. Killy opened the rear of the armored car and helped stow the crate inside.

"Where are we going?" Cheroff demanded.

"Safety."

Cheroff watched more fire trucks leaving the camp

and ran back inside, bringing out more crates. Finally, he emerged with two bulging briefcases, and after him came Maria.

"Quickly, quickly." Cheroff pushed his wife before she could get a good look at Killy. They climbed in with the crates and Killy locked them in. He got behind the wheel.

"Good work, Tovarisch," he heard Gogol's voice behind him in grudging, mocking compliment.

At the north gate, the massed tanks and infantry were looking out, not in. Killy passed through with a wave, away from the camp and tilled fields and into the cold dark of the Manchurian desert. A mile from the sentries, he shut off his headlights but kept his speed. The Chinese were bound to put up helicopters.

The grate that provided communication between the rear of the car and Killy slid open.

"We're going north. That's to the Russian border," Cheroff inquired.

"Orders."

"General Li's orders?"

Killy didn't answer.

"I don't understand," Cheroff grumbled. "Maria, you speak Chinese better. See if you can get this man to talk."

A new face appeared at the grate. She started to talk and then her mouth shut. Killy caught her eyes traveling over his smile.

"I understand," she sighed.

She slid the grate shut.

TWENTY-TWO

IT WAS DAWN. The armored car sat hidden by scrub in a dry riverbed. There had been no water in the river since spring, and the tracks of wild dromedaries that had come to drink months before pocked the hard soil. A PLA helicopter passed by a mile away. Gogol kept his automatic on the Cheroffs until the helicopter was gone and then put it away and returned to a breakfast of soybean bars.

"So you're an Inquisitor," he said to Killy. "A holy agent. That explains a lot."

"He specializes in his own resurrection," Maria Cheroff remarked.

"You resurrect pretty well, too," Killy replied. "Moscow, Kansas, China. How long have you been in contact with Li?"

"For a year," she answered blandly. "After our friends in Moscow failed to protect us, we had to look around for new patrons, and we found them in the Lin Pao clique."

Lin Pao had been commander of the PLA and heir

to Mao until his assassination, leaving the generals under him leaderless and unhappy. Since then, Peking had systematically lopped off members of the clique; Liu Hsing-yuan in Kwantung, Liang Hsing-chu in Szechwan, Air Force Commander Wu Fahsien, Navy political commissar Li Two-pang, Deputy Chief of Staff Chiu Hui-tso, and Yeh Chun, Lin's wife. Maria rattled off their names without concern.

"All that mattered to us was that they use my husband's methods. They wanted proof of success and he gave it to them in Kansas. In another month or two months, they would have been ready to move against Peking."

"Now I go back a prisoner to Russia," Cheroff said. "And all I ever wanted was to prove my technique, to show that individuals can be conditioned for or against violence as society sees fit. For the betterment of the greater number, isn't that the tenet of Soviet medicine?"

"It's a little late to turn philosophical," Killy suggested.

Maria patted her husband's hand. Their night trip had been rough, covering over 100 miles of hard desert without lights. The stars led them north to the Amur River and the Russian border, but only Killy and Gogol could see the stars. The Cheroffs had been caged inside the armored vehicle.

Fatigue had eroded the scientist's confidence but not Maria's. She was still as calm and as beautiful as when Killy first met her. Since then, throughout the recuperation in Rome and the journey to Moscow, he had wondered why he let her take him in. Seeing her again told him why.

"I've wondered," she asked him. "How did you manage to fight the patterning? You were Alex's only failure."

"I was used to military men," Cheroff muttered. "Officers work in patterns, follow orders. I needed more time with him, another day and I could have done it."

"Maybe," Killy granted.

Gogol studied a map.

"We will move out again tonight. The Chinese know we're going to the border, but they don't know if we're heading for the border along the Amur River or the Ussuri River. It's about two hundred miles either direction. They'll have to spread out their search. We can make it to the Amur in two days and crack the Chinese line."

How they would do that, Gogol didn't say. The Russians and Chinese had been carrying on a sporadic war along the Amur for a year, and the border was heavily defended by tanks and artillery. There were times when Killy wished the quarreling progeny of Lenin got along a little better.

"One more day, and you would have been mine," Cheroff mused as he gazed at Killy.

They subsisted on soybean cakes and tea until dark covered the desert. The Cheroffs were locked inside the armored car, Gogol took his post at the gun and Killy drove. An hour after they had started out, Killy killed the engine and they stood and watched a convoy of Chinese jeeps and personnel carriers pass by on the right. He started again at an angle away from the searchers.

Out of the wastelands of Mongolia and Manchuria had come the nomads who conquered China and half of Europe. The nomads were gone but the wasteland remained, sun-baked flats stretching the distance of

Rome to Paris or New York to Chicago.

An hour before dawn, he stopped the car again. The long line of searchers was returning more than half a mile away, their lights on for greater speed.

"They've given up," Gogol said. "They wouldn't have their lights on if they weren't giving up."

Killy counted the vehicles. Each one was accounted for. The Russian was right.

"And just fifty miles to the river from here," Gogol added. "Just fifty miles to Russia and the Cheroffs are ours."

"And we leave his notes and equipment in the river," Killy answered.

"That was our agreement, Inquisitor. I personally will deal with the Cheroffs."

A mile on they found a thicket of brush and Killy drove in the middle of it. The car had no more than stopped when he fell asleep for the first time in sixty hours.

A lizard woke him up. Escaping the cold of the early morning, it crawled in the front of the armored car and up Killy's sleeve, dragging itself to his armpit, where it rolled into a ball. Killy refrained from hitting the animal, sliding his hand in, instead, and rubbing the lizard's silky stomach. When the lizard was thoroughly numbed with pleasure, Killy took it out of his shirt and stepped outside the car to let the desert dweller free.

Gogol was not in the turret. Killy opened the rear of the car. The Cheroffs were gone. Still inside were the crates. Killy lifted the covers off. His stomach tightened as he saw the familiar skull harness, leather and metal sockets fashioned into an unearthly helmet. Not a helmet, he corrected himself. Cheroff's brainchild, the personality overrider, the key to the soul created from electrodes and tortured nerves. He let the lid down gingerly, admitting his fear.

The second crate contained the lasers and generator. The third crate, the heaviest, held batteries.

When the Russians returned before dawn, Killy was asleep again.

"Killy, that is your real name, isn't it?" Gogol shook his arm. "Wake up. Have some breakfast."

Cheroff was in the back, checking his equipment. Maria warmed tea over a fire.

"I must have been dead." Killy scratched the stubble on his chin.

"We already had a morning stroll." Gogol slapped Killy's back. "Tea has caffeine. It'll wake you up. We have a lot to do today."

The two agents and their captives sat around the cozy fire. Gogol was in a cheery mood and described his race with Killy through Gorky Park.

"I heard you killed my husband's assistant." Maria refilled Killy's cup.

"How many men have you killed by remote control?" he asked as he took it.

"Necessary experiments, not murder. And they weren't saints," she said lightly. "Just as you weren't."

"But no killer, not if he can help it," Gogol contributed. "I found out on the train. Among agents, almost a saint. Killy, would you like to know how we go over the river?"

"Very much."

Gogol took his gun from his jacket and laid it on the ground. Using a stick, he drew a line in front of the gun. Every five inches along the line in the dirt, he put a stone.

"The line is the Amur River. There is no fishing on this stretch, so the Chinese have a wire fence, according to Doctor Cheroff. Every two hundred yards there is a watchtower and every ten miles there is an infantry and armored company. The one point of access over the river is a ferry landing. It's no longer used since the hostilities, but the Chinese guard it in case an attack is made from the other side."

He pushed the gun toward the line.

"Now we have wire cutters in the car to get through the fence, but we need a distraction to give us time. That means one of us must drive the car directly at the guards at the ferry to draw their attention."

"Their fire," Killy corrected them.

"Their fire, then."

"And who would be fool enough to do that?"

"Isn't it obvious?"

Gogol picked up the gun and aimed it at Killy's chest.

"You see, I was the contact in the KGB for the Cheroffs. Unfortunately, during the investigations Alex became frightened and ran from the Center, using me to get him out of the country, then changing his face and vanishing without a trace. The man you set on fire was running to me for help. I had to shoot him before he said anything. I would have shot you also but there were too many others watching us by then. After you spoke to my superiors, I had no choice but accompany you to China."

"The girls were sent to kill you."

Gogol grinned. "Alex still didn't trust me. I've finally convinced him to, and why not? With the proven success of his techniques outside the Soviet Union, he can have his own laboratory, cars, a large apartment and a dacha in the country. We will be heros, thanks to your destruction of the missile. You thought you were using me. I was using you. That's all that happened. Alex, will you get your equipment?"

Cheroff brought the harness out of the car and set the lasers in them. Killy felt his hair stand on end.

"It didn't work before."

Cheroff attached electrical wires from the laser tubes to the generator and hooked the generator into the batteries. He twisted the generator's single knob and watched the rheostat needle jump.

"Everything is in working order," he said.

"Nothing will fail this time, Jean Mainz," Maria explained. "Last time our control wore off between patterning sessions. The end of your life will be one long patterning session."

Her eyes were dark as sapphires but harder.

"I wonder," Killy mused. "Up till now I think there was some adolescent part of my head that still thought it was rescuing you."

His words went by her like a love poem past a statue.

"Put it there." Gogol pointed with his gun. "Let him put it on by himself."

Cheroff set the harness on the ground and stepped back.

"I won't do it," Killy said.

"You will or I'll kill you now," the Russian agent answered him. "I'd rather leave you dead than have you alive."

Killy picked up the harness.

"On your head," Gogol ordered.

Killy took off his Chinese cap and set the harness in its place. Each motion was distilled by fear. His scalp crawled under the feel of the leather. His fingers drew the strap tight under his chin and buckled it. He felt his aorta squeezing and gulping blood. Sound was muffled by the harness, but his eyes saw everything with that sickening clarity of texture that always came with fever.

"I want to see it work," Gogol said.

He wasn't healed, Killy knew, as soon as the laser's flash sliced open his brain. The center of that treacherous gray mass was still raw and more vulnerable than before. He stumbled and fell to his knees, tried to cry and couldn't. His face was twisted in a mute grimace of pain, and the laughter of the Russians merged with the insistent, overwhelming pulse of the fire in his skull.

TWENTY-THREE

THE AMUR IS a Siberian river, an ice-floe-choked strip of water between flat banks. Alex Cheroff clutched his briefcases full of notes as he squirmed through a grasping thicket of tundra brush. Ahead was the fence, and 300 yards to the side was the ferry landing. A bored platoon of Chinese soldiers loitered there with the crews of two light tanks.

Gogol listened for the sound of the armored car.

"He will do as you say?" he asked.

"He is wearing the harness, so he has no choice. He'll do what I told him."

Cheroff's confidence overcame his chattering teeth. Maria kissed his cheek.

"Once we're on the other side, everything will be all right," she reassured him. "They'll only fire in the water, not to the other side."

"Shh. I hear him." Gogol raised his hand.

The soldiers at the landing heard the car, too, but the road wound through scrub trees and they couldn't see it. The car was traveling fast, though, as Cheroff ordered, and the Russian crept closer to the fence.

The armored car burst from the trees. The soldiers knew at once it wasn't going to stop. The tanks converged to block the gate. An officer waved his arms.

Gogol was already at the fence, using his cutter. Cold had made the fence wire slippery. When he cut the first wire it sang.

"Hurry," Cheroff pleaded.

Rifle fire bounced off the car's armor and bullet-proof glass. A tank shuddered as it fired its cannon. The shell missed the car and plowed a row through the trees.

Gogol's wire cutter grew blunt. He tore at the last almost severed wire and forced it free. Cheroff was the first one through. Maria and Gogol slid down the bank after him.

The car careened around another shell. Soldiers ran behind the tanks. They didn't need to. The third cannon shell ripped through the armored car's engine and out the back. An explosion followed a moment later, funnels of flame shooting out the turret and windows. The soldiers approached it, one or two taking cautious shots. When they ceased, the burning wreck looked like an anticlimax for so much excitement. They were ready for a fight now and the fight was over.

Cheroff hung onto his notes and Gogol and Maria pulled him through the water. The ice floes offered protection but they were also dangerous, white hulks as heavy as locomotives and some sharp as glass. Part of one floe snapped off by Cheroff's head.

"They see us. Just keep your heads down," Gogol ordered. "When we get to the other side, we're safe. There must be Russians coming by now."

More shots followed from the ferry. A tank turned

its cannon to the water but by then it was too late. Three figures were dragging themselves up on the far bank. The Chinese stopped firing, cheated twice.

"I did it," Gogol gasped. "I brought you back."

Cheroff was bent over his briefcases. His beard was already beginning to frost. Maria lay on the bank, crying with relief. The snap of an AK-47 safety sliding free brought her head up.

"I knew you could do it," Killy said. He stepped out from the trees and relieved Gogol of his automatic. Killy was as wet as they were, but his rifle was dry.

The Cheroffs gaped.

"How?" Gogol asked.

"While you were out on your morning stroll, I drained the laser batteries and adjusted the generator needle. It was only good for a few real jolts."

The explanation sank slowly into an exhausted Cheroff. He rocked back and forth on his knees. Gogol judged the odds of grabbing the submachine gun.

"Don't try it," Killy advised him. "After all, you left it for me to use in my glorious crash. Well, the car went on without me and I used your hole in the fence."

Gogol blew water out of his nose.

"It wouldn't have been hard to reach here before we dragged this coward across the river."

"My equipment destroyed for nothing," Cheroff moaned.

"That's all right," Maria comforted him. "You still have your notes. You can build more."

She pressed her husband's head between her breasts and patted his cheek. The scene was pathetic and grotesque enough to stop Killy for a moment.

"I'm afraid not," he said.

He ripped the briefcases from Cheroff's hands. The scientist watched, horrified, as Killy threw the first briefcase fifty feet into the river. Waterlogged, the briefcase sank. Killy threw the second nearer because it broke open in mid-air. Papers sailed over the surface of the water.

"His life's work. You're ruining it all," Maria screamed.

Killy tried to stop her, but Maria evaded his hand and plunged into the river, wading out to the floating papers. The ice floes pulled at her, trying to drag her down.

"Come back, they see you!" Killy yelled.

Cheroff dove after his wife. Killy thought the doctor would drag her back to shore. Instead, he began collecting the effluvia of pages, too, stuffing them in his pockets. Maria's head submerged and reappeared.

"Come back!"

Muzzle flashes sparkled along the Chinese side of the Amur. From reflex Killy and Gogol spread-eagled on the ground. The water around the Cheroffs shot up in geysers, but Killy could still make them out intently gathering disintegrating scraps of notes, the sum total of their lives. The sound of sucking air preceded a tank shell.

A wave of water deluged the two men on the bank. Killy swallowed and got his hearing back. The Chinese had stopped firing; they were cheering. Where the Cheroffs had been was a wide circle of bare water. There were no ice floes, not even the smallest bits of paper and not a trace of a man or a woman. Already new ice floes moved in to fill the vacuum and cover the grave.

"Gone," Killy muttered. He got to his feet. What was there to cheer about?

"Yes," Gogol said, "but I still have you. An Inquisitor isn't too bad a catch. Russian troops will be here any second after that noise. You can't escape, so you're mine."

"Every cloud a silver lining? Sorry, I won't need to escape. I'll take your identification, be generally unpleasant and I should pass as you."

Gogol laughed and got to his feet. He put his hand out for the submachine gun.

"Another man would, not you. Not a man from the Vatican."

Killy stepped back but Gogol went around him, forcing him to the river.

"Just give me a day's lead, Gogol."

"I won't give you anything. I'll take the rifle. Hear that sound? Russian tanks."

The Chinese watched with glasses from their side of the river. Incredibly, the two fugitives still alive seemed to be fighting. Each had a hand on the submachine gun between them and then the rifle came alive. The fugitive at the wrong end staggered and spun around and around before he hit the ground. Even through the glasses, the Chinese were able to catch the dead man's look of surprise.

"Just a day's lead," Killy asked.

Gogol said nothing and stared blindly at the sky. His coat was turning a darker black. Killy knelt beside Gogol and slid his lids shut. From Gogol's pocket he took a pigskin billfold and opened it to a card bearing the dead man's identification and picture. Water had warped the photo almost past recognition. When he'd put the billfold in his own pocket, Killy grabbed Gogol's ankles and dragged him to the edge of the bank.

"Unto Almighty God we commend the soul of our brother departed, and we commit his body to the deep." Killy bowed his head, which directed his eyes to the last, long look at the dead man. "Oh, the hell with it."

He gave Gogol a firm shove with his foot and sent him into the water. Killy stood on the bank and waited until ice floes surrounded and hid the body.

A noise of gears and breaking branches came through the trees. Killy stepped briskly off to meet the tanks. He hoped nothing went wrong getting back to Rome; his penance was adding up.

BURNT OFFERINGS

A novel by
ROBERT MARASCO

WHEN MARIAN ROLFE FOUND THE LISTING IN
THE WANT ADS, IT SEEMED ALMOST TOO GOOD TO
BE TRUE:

> *Unique summer home. Restful, secluded.
> Perfect for large family. Pool, private
> beach, dock. Long season. Very reason-
> able for the right people.*

AND THE ROLFES WERE THE RIGHT PEOPLE.
MARIAN KNEW IT THE SECOND SHE FELT HERSELF
SURROUNDED BY THE AUBUSSONS AND CRYSTAL.
AS FOR BEN, HIS DOUBTS ABOUT SOME "CATCH"
SEEMED SILLY. UNTIL, STEP BY STEP, THE HOUSE
AND GROUNDS BEGAN TO EXERT THEIR POWER AND
PLUNGE THE ROLFES INTO A NIGHTMARE OF
EXQUISITELY MOUNTING HORROR.

A DELL BOOK $1.50

"unusual, gripping and menacing"
—*New York Times*

SHOOT

by DOUGLAS FAIRBAIRN

"*This is what happened. Myself and four friends were hunting along the Stirrup River one weekend in the deer season . . . when we noticed that there was another party of deer hunters standing on the opposite bank . . . Then, all of a sudden, without any warning and I swear to God without any provocation from us, one of them raised his rifle and fired, hitting Pete Rinaldi in the head . . .*"

From that spare beginning, this gripping tale of violence moves through the unfulfilled lives of its small-town war veterans, their sex-entanglements and gun fantasies, to a full-scale mini-war.

"Like James Dickey's superb novel, *"Deliverance,"* 'SHOOT' is about the American male's quest for manhood through violence and sex."
—*Tuscaloosa News*

"A tough, fast-moving chiller right up to the terrible climax."
—*Jackson Daily News*

A DELL BOOK $1.50
Soon to be a major Columbia movie

THE TAKING OF PELHAM ONE TWO THREE

a novel by
John Godey

If you cannot obtain copies of this title from your local bookseller, just send the price (plus 25¢ per copy for handling and postage) to Dell Books, Post Office Box 1000, Pinebrook, N. J. 07058.

HOW MANY OF THESE DELL BESTSELLERS HAVE YOU READ?